"What's bugging you, Sal?" he asked softly. "You're not yourself."

"Maybe that's the problem."

"What do you mean?"

"I don't know," I said, still uptight and not wanting to talk about it.

"Look, lambchop," he said, pulling me close to him, "whenever you do want to talk, I'm here."

"I know," I said, grateful that he wasn't chewing me out for being such a deadhead all night.

"I love you, Sal," he whispered, and gently pressed my head against his shoulder. Ordinarily, he would have begun kissing me, but he sensed that I just wanted to be held. For the longest time we stayed there while he stroked my hair and I clung to him.

"Remember, you can always count on me," he said.

THE
SEARCHING HEART

Patricia Aks

FAWCETT JUNIPER • NEW YORK

For Barbara Lowenstein

Chapter 1.

For as long as I can remember, I've known I was adopted, but lately that's all I can think about. My preoccupation with who my real parents are began at the beginning of September when my English teacher, Miss Johnson—no Ms. for her—gave us one of her famous writing assignments. This time we were to write a thousand words on "Who Am I?"

Miss Johnson, obviously unmarried or anything, looks like an old-fashioned schoolmarm—tall, skinny, plain—but she has a reputation for being everybody's favorite English teacher, even for those kids who never thought they liked to read. She only teaches high school, so I didn't have her until tenth grade, and the first day of class I could see she was an original. She asked each of us what we'd read over the summer, and everyone mentioned one or two books. Some of us may have been faking it, but it would have

1

been too embarrassing not to mention at least one title. Only Arthur, six feet two, one eighty, Greek god looks, super-jock and A-one wiseguy, had nothing to report.

"I never read in the summer," he said, deadpanned.

"You mean you never read unless something's assigned?" Miss Johnson asked evenly.

"Right."

"I think you have a serious problem, Arthur, but I also think I have a cure." She pulled a paperback book out of her desk drawer and held it up. "This is a collection of Roald Dahl short stories. I have cut out the last half of every story, and I am giving you this as an assignment. You must read the first half, and then tell me at our next class if you honestly don't care about reading the endings."

"Okay," he said, catching the truncated copy she tossed to him. "But I'm sure I can resist."

"There's only one person you'll be hurting if you do," she said, and then turned to the rest of us. "I don't usually go around ripping up books, but in this case the cure is *not* worse than the disease. And I've had one hundred percent success in treating this ailment in the past."

We all cracked up, and even Arthur had to smile. Then Miss Johnson suggested that the rest of us read the whole book so that we would understand why her method of treating "voluntary illiteracy" was so effective. With that buildup, I couldn't wait to get my hands on the collection, and of course she was absolutely right. It would have been a form of torture to read half a Roald Dahl story. And Arthur announced at our next English class that Miss Johnson had actually changed his whole attitude about reading—possibly changed his whole life—and then sheepishly pleaded with her to let him have the missing pages. The class applauded Arthur's surprising reaction, a beatific smile spread across Miss Johnson's face, and she muttered, "Another soul saved."

I know it sounds dramatic, but after that day Arthur became less conceited, more likable. It supported a theory I'd been developing that a single incident can change one's whole life. I couldn't wait to tell Nina, who always kids me about my theories, and accuses me of being an incurable romantic philosopher. I call her the "ultimate pragmatist."

Nina and I have been friends since we were five years old, even though we're very different. In kindergarten during "free time" she would build skyscrapers with blocks while I painted watercolors of sailboats and sunsets. Even then, we shared one interest in common: music. She played the tambourine and I played the triangle, and we always missed the beat and had uncontrollable giggling fits. Now we're both in the school orchestra. She plays the flute and I play the violin and fortunately we don't miss the beat very often, but we still, even at fifteen, have occasional laughing spasms.

One of my theories that Nina agrees with is that our similar sense of humor has enabled us to be best friends for more than half of our lives. In a way, that's a miracle because not only is she practical and precise, while I tend to be dreamy and vague, but she knows exactly when she wants to do with her life, which is be a doctor. She's a whiz at math and science—my worst subjects—but she comes by it rightly. Her father is a prominent neurosurgeon, her mother is a chemist, and her brother is a premed student at the University of Michigan. That bears out another one of my recent theories: that genes, as well as environment, determine what one does in life, especially genes. Otherwise, I'd be good at math too, because my father—my adoptive father, George—teaches math at our school. George teases me about everything, especially about

3

how I might ruin his reputation if I fail in his subject. But I've never gotten less than a C plus, even in algebra, so he knows he's safe, although his talent with numbers never rubbed off on me.

Nina did concede a few days after the Arthur incident that he had definitely improved. We were walking home from school after orchestra rehearsal, and she admitted that Arthur seemed much less arrogant and bored in class. He participated in some of the discussions and no longer slumped in his chair in a world-weary manner. But Nina claimed he was heading in that direction anyway.

"He was looking for an excuse to get off his high horse, and Miss Johnson gave it to him. It would have happened anyway."

"You mean it wasn't just because she encouraged him to admit publicly that he wanted to read."

"I don't think so. I believe he was ripe for change, and if this hadn't triggered it, something else would have."

We had arrived at the intersection where we take opposite directions. I live on Netherlands Avenue in a small gray clapboard house surrounded by similar-looking houses on a tree-lined block. Nina's house was built on a hill on Rivers Road and overlooks the Hudson River.

I didn't think too much more about our discussion until a week later when Miss Johnson gave us the "Who Am I?" assignment. Answering that question seemed easy on the surface. As Miss Johnson pointed out, "me" is everyone's favorite subject. We had a week to complete it, but I was actually looking forward to writing my autobiography and I began the Monday it was assigned.

It had been an ordinary day. We'd had spaghetti and meatballs for dinner, which I had prepared because I was the first one home. George had to stay after school for a faculty meeting, and Lucy, my mother, had one of her full

4

days at the real estate office where she works three days a week.

Lucy had always been a homemaker until last summer, when she decided to earn some extra money. She calls it the "fun fund," but I know it's mainly money she's earning so that I can go to whatever college I choose. Lucy never lays any guilt on me, and goes out of her way to tell me how much she enjoys showing houses. When she made her first commission last summer, she blew us to a French dinner at a well-known restaurant in Connecticut. The bill was astronomical, but she paid it gleefully.

"We can't do this too often," George remarked smiling, "or there won't be anything left for Sally."

Lucy shot him a "shut-up" look and emoted about the coffee mousse, which she planned to duplicate as soon as she determined the secret ingredient. George seemed slightly chagrined, and I realized then that although Lucy did enjoy working, she was mainly doing it for me. One of the results of Lucy being out of the house all day is that I have more responsibility in the kitchen. I'm not crazy about cooking, but Lucy and George always rave so much about whatever I concoct that it's well worth the effort. The truth is, they think everything I do is special. I've never had the usual hassles that most my friends have with their parents. I suppose I took that for granted, the way one takes good health for granted. I mean if you have a cold in the nose or a splinter in your hand, that's all you can think about, but no one carries on about how well one feels.

It wasn't until I sat down at my typewriter and started banging out some random notes that I planned to organize later into a finished paper that I viewed myself objectively. I began with the vital statistics: My name is Sally Brighton, born June 10, 1968, and adopted two days later by Lucy and George. Understandably, I don't look at all like my parents. I'm five three, one hundred and two, straight long auburn hair, dark brown eyes. Lucy has short curly blond hair, hazel-colored eyes, is over five feet eight, and when her weight is down wears a size 12. Lucy's personality reflects her looks: hearty, loving, warm. George has sandy hair, mild blue eyes, an average build, and his easy-going, unpretentious manner belies his razor-sharp mind.

George, who has been a teacher at the private coed school in Riverdale, New York, where I have been a student since kindergarten, reluctantly wears the required jacket and tie to work. As soon as he gets home, he changes into jeans and a T-shirt. He is addicted to mystery books, crossword puzzles, and an occasional beer. Weekends he spends puttering in our tiny garden in back of our house, where he's planted one patch of vegetables and one of flowers, or else refinishing furniture.

I rambled on about how my parents rarely argued and that I had this really good relationship with them. My father's unable to express his feelings the way Lucy can, but I know how much I mean to him. Sometimes I catch him looking at me and smiling, and the look on his face tells it all. My mother, on the other hand, will sometimes stop in the middle of whatever she's doing—cleaning up the dishes, drying her hair, or writing out a grocery list—to remark how lucky she is to have me for a daughter.

Then I went on to describe Nina, who is at least three inches taller than me, beautifully proportioned, graceful as a cat, and totally unaware of her golden classic looks. Nina has it all, as far as I can see, beauty and brains, but she's not the least bit snobby. When her father was appointed head of the neurosurgery department of a prestigious hospital in New York, there was a half-page article on him in the local newspaper. Nina, instead of being pleased, confided to me that she almost didn't go to school the day the article appeared because she was so embarrassed by the publicity. When some kids did comment on it, she did everything possible to change the subject.

Besides my parents and Nina, the most important person in my life is Eric Lawrence. He's been my boyfriend for almost a year, and though we're not officially committed to going steady, he's the only boy I go out with, and vice versa.

Eric is a head taller than me and has a neat athletic build, and I find him very attractive. However, if you analyze his features, he isn't at all handsome. He has unruly black hair, dark eyes, pale skin, a narrow acquiline nose, and a too wide mouth. He looks more like Al Pacino than Robert Redford, but he has a devastating smile, and although he's only a year older than me, he's much more mature.

Eric is from a very affluent family. His father is a senior partner in a prominent New York investment firm, and his mother is the daughter of a leading soap manufacturer in the Midwest, but Eric is amazingly indifferent to his background. He rarely goes to the posh country club where his family are members. I've been his guest there a number of times and I have to agree that the air there is too rarified and there are too many rules. Not even *off*-white is allowed on the tennis courts, and jeans are unacceptable. Eric prefers hanging out at the public beaches or playing tennis on the school courts.

We're both camera freaks and got to know each other last year at the photography club. Eric specializes in architectural photography and I'm mainly interested in nature shots. It was after one of the meetings that we became friendly. It wasn't exactly moonlight and roses in the darkroom—more the aroma of chemicals than the fragrance of mimosa—but it was cozy and we unavoidably kept bumping into each other. I was a novice at developing pictures, and he gave me a number of pointers on how to bring out detail. When I was dumping my film in the developing solution, it seemed like the most natural thing in the world for him to put his hand on my shoulder. We lost all track of time, and the security guard had to unlock the front door so that we could leave. We broke up thinking about the scandal we would have caused if we'd been trapped in school overnight.

Eric walked me home and we rapped all the way about photography. When we arrived at my house, I stopped before the path leading to the front door and summed up what we'd been saying: "I guess we agree that there's the excitement of freezing on film a memorable fleeting moment, whether it's the petals of a flower opening, or the way the light bounces off a building."

"Hey," Eric said, "you're not only pretty, you're a poet!"

No boy had ever complimented me like that before and I didn't know what to say. I mumbled something inane about having to hurry, and although my legs suddenly felt weak, they managed to propel me up the path to my door. Eric waited while I fumbled with my key and let myself in. When I turned to wave good-bye, it was already dusk, but even from a distance that dazzling smile came through.

I was in a daze the rest of the evening. All I could think about was Eric, Eric, Eric. My mother wanted to know if I was feeling okay because I barely ate any of a favorite dish she'd prepared, coq au vin. And when my father finally got my attention—he had to ask me to pass the butter three times—he made some remark about me acting as though I had had a religious experience. I grinned foolishly, made some ridiculous reference to how I'd mastered the finer points of developing film, and volunteered to do the dishes. Just then the phone rang, and Lucy went into the kitchen to pick up the receiver.

"It's for you, Sally. Says he's Eric and he hopes he isn't interrupting our dinner."

I leapt out of my chair so quickly I barely missed tipping over my water glass. "I'll take it upstairs," I said, flying away from the table.

"Don't worry about the dishes," Lucy called after me.

That was fortunate, because forty minutes later I was still on the phone, and when I finally came downstairs my parents were in the living room watching the news. Tactfully, they didn't quiz me about the call, and I sank down on the floor pillow and stared at the TV screen. I didn't have the vaguest idea what the commentator was talking about. I was too busy trying to remember my exact conversation with Eric. But I realized when the program was over because my father got up from his black leather chair and flipped off the set.

"Who's for Scrabble?" he asked, glancing at my mother, who was concentrating on her knitting.

"Not me," Lucy answered. "If I don't finish this sweater in two weeks, it'll be late for Judy's birthday."

"You can always give it to her for Christmas," George suggested.

"Don't be funny, dear. It's my sister's fortieth, and it's got to be special."

"How about you, Sal? You game for a game?"

"Huh?" I hadn't been listening.

"Never mind," George sighed. "This was just a ploy for me to postpone correcting papers."

"Uh huh," I said vaguely. "And I think I better do my homework."

I pulled myself up and slowly trod up the stairs. I was

sure my parents weren't aware of what I was going through, but then I heard Lucy say to George, "You know something? I think Sally's in love."

"Lucy, that's exactly what I was thinking."

They obviously thought I was out of earshot, but I couldn't help calling downstairs.

"I've got news for you both: you're right!"

Chapter 2.

When Miss Johnson had assigned us the "Who Am I?" paper, she had told us to be as personal as we wished. Then she added, "Although I think it's valuable to read papers aloud in class, in this case I can understand why you may not want to share your private lives with everyone. Therefore, simply write 'confidential' at the top of your title page, and I promise to respect your wishes. It's much more important for you to gain insights into yourself than it is to write a bland essay suitable for public consumption."

I polished up my rambling, expanded on some early childhood memories, none of them notable, and described our summers. George worked as a swimming coach at the local Y and I waited tables at the Shadow Box, a moderate-priced restaurant in our neighborhood. The highlight of our summer for the past six years was our three-week vacation in the Adirondacks, where we rented a cabin on a lake.

Before typing up the final version, I decided to wait a day. I'd learned long ago that what I regarded as deathless prose immediately after I'd written it seemed more like warmed-over hash when I reread it twenty-four hours later. Also, it would be easier for me to be objective if I waited a day. Therefore, it wasn't until the following evening that I settled down to evaluate as objectively as possible what I had written. When I was finished, I knew it was passable—the events of my life were in sequence and I'd been honest about saying what was important to me—but I knew there was something wrong. I read it through three more times, looking for the flaw, and then it hit me. Except for a superficial description, it didn't at all answer the question, "Who Am I?"

I thought perhaps I'd held back writing about the *real* me because even though Miss Johnson had assured us our papers would remain confidential if that was our preference, maybe I didn't want to reveal myself, warts and all, even to her.

I put the paper aside, pushed back my chair, and looked around my room as though that would provide me with some answers. My room is on the small side, but I love it. George made built-ins that cover one wall and combine bookshelves, a desk, and drawers. For my fifteenth birthday, one of his presents was to let me select a wallpaper that he would hang. I chose a tiny rosebud pattern, Lucy whipped up a rose-colored cotton spread for my high-rise bed—when the bottom bed is pulled out there is absolutely no floor space—and I hemmed a sheer gauzy material for the window.

I have three prints that I developed, close-ups of wild flowers, above my bed, a silver-framed snapshot of Eric on my night table next to a well-thumbed copy of poems by Emily Dickenson, and a white wicker rocking chair where Ermantrude sits. Ermantrude, the last vestige of my childhood, is a tattered, scruffy Teddy bear, who I can't seem to discard. I've had Ermantrude as long as I can remember, and he played a major part in my very first memory. There was a tiny rubber inflatable pool filled with a few inches of water in our backyard, and I was still a toddler but I remember distinctly insisting that he had to go swimming and my parents protesting and me plunging him into the water and then all of us laughing.

I thought perhaps I should include that anecdote in my paper, not because it was so unusual but because from the very beginning Lucy and George doted on me and found humor in a situation that would have made most parents angry. Still, seeing myself in relationship with Lucy and George, no matter how far back I went or how clearly I perceived it, didn't tell me who I was. I had this crazy notion that I should call Nina or Eric and ask them if they had any ideas on the subject, but I knew they wouldn't take me seriously. Besides, it was only Tuesday and I still had six days before my paper was due. By then I might come up with some brilliant insights. For the time being I would just stop thinking about it. The greatest distraction for me was to play around with my photographs.

I took a box of recently developed pictures out of my drawer. Since I had had access to the darkroom at school, I always had a zillion prints that needed sorting out. But after fifteen minutes of waffling over which ones to keep in my album, possibly frame, or throw out, I decided to take a bath and go to bed. This obviously wasn't one of my more productive days.

Soaking in the tub usually makes me totally mindless, but I couldn't dispel a vague feeling of unease. And no matter how hard I tried, the "Who Am I?" question would not stay on the back burner. I went through the ritual of bathing and toweling off, and decided I couldn't put off talking to Nina, even if she made fun of me. She'd always come through for me in the past, and I could count on her being 100 percent direct.

My parents were downstairs, so I could use the phone in their room in privacy. I put on my nightshirt, grabbed my paper, hurried into their room, and dialed Nina's number. She not only has her own phone but she also has her own private line. She picked up the receiver immediately and I plunged right in, telling her my dissatisfaction with what I'd written.

"Read it to me," she said.

I rapidly reeled off my paper, which did sound adequate even to my critical ears, and then waited for her response.

"Why are you making such a big deal of this?" she asked. "You've done the assignment and it's fine. I haven't even started mine, and it'll probably be boring by comparison."

"At least you can write about wanting to be a doctor, and knowing where you're going and all that."

"You and I both know that most kids our age don't have the foggiest idea what they're going to do in life. I guess I'm lucky that I do know, but that's not what you called about. I can assure you, Sally, that your autobiography is perfectly okay and you should stop worrying."

"What bothers me has nothing to do with the writing. It has to do with the subject matter: my identity."

"But you've said who you are. Sally Brighton, fifteen years old, et cetera, et cetera."

"I've said what I am, but not who. I can't really know that unless I know where I came from."

"You came from your mother, dummy."

"I know that, but who is she? And who is my father?"

There was a long pause, and then Nina, who is seldom at a loss for words, muttered softly, "Who knows?"

"I sure don't," I said, "and I'll probably never find out. But now I know what's been bothering me, and it's almost a relief. You see, I can't really know myself if I don't know my real parents."

"Your *biological* parents," Nina explained scientifically.

"Exactly. And since that's not about to happen, I might as well be satisfied with my paper and go to sleep."

"Good thinking. And while you're in dreamland, I'll be reviewing French idioms for a test we have tomorrow."

"I'm sorry if I tore you away from your homework."

"*Au contraire*, you did me a favor. I was hoping there would be an interruption, and I thank you."

"I know you're kidding, Nina, but I really do thank you for all your help."

"All I did was assure you that you wrote a decent paper."

"You have no idea what you did."

"Sometimes, Sally, I don't know what you're talking about, but now is not the time for me to figure it out. Sweet dreams!"

"Sweet dreams," I echoed, hung up the receiver, and slowly returned to my room, totally bemused by our conversation.

It was amazing that something so obvious had escaped me. How could I pretend to know myself if I knew nothing about my heredity? And even more surprising was the fact that I'd lived fifteen years and not been at all concerned about my roots. It didn't seem possible that a simple writing assignment in English could stir up so many buried thoughts and feelings.

As I drifted off to sleep, I recalled Nina's comment about Arthur, who we both agreed had definitely improved after Miss Johnson's treatment. "He was ripe for change. If this hadn't triggered it, something else would."

Was that true of me? Was it inevitable that I would want to find out about my origins? The whole idea was unnerving—scary and exciting at the same time—and intuitively I knew that pursuing it would cause a great deal of pain. It wouldn't be worth upsetting the lives of everyone I was closest to, and I resolved to keep these gnawing questions to myself.

Chapter 3.

Through the next few weeks I found myself making resolutions. Making resolutions is easy—think of all the noble plans one makes on New Year's Eve—but keeping them is something else. I had never dwelt on the issue of my adoption, although I never kept it a secret, and that was probably the case because Lucy and George were so comfortable with the idea. Except for a few insensitive remarks made by kids when I was about five or six years old, I was never disturbed by the fact. I remember a bratty first-grader with whom I was playing hopscotch announcing in a loud voice in the middle of the game, "You're 'dopted, you know. You don't live with your real mother and father."

"So what?" I answered, and went right on with my turn.

It's clear to me now that because my reaction was so

cool, she, and everyone around us who was expecting a fight, was disappointed. If anything, my status with the group improved.

I was only a little kid then and I could handle knowing I was adopted. But at fifteen, with ten years more living experience, I no longer had a "so-what" attitude. I was fighting desperately to keep my vow not to involve anyone else in what was beginning to dominate my thoughts, but I was losing ground in that battle. I found myself making oblique references to adoption in situations that didn't remotely call for it. I became aware of this tendency one day when I was having a Coke with Nina and my two other closest friends, Chris and Bambi.

It was our Friday ritual to meet at Nick's, a hamburger joint by day disguised as a discotheque at night, and discuss life. We made a concerted effort not to talk about boys, and we did have some amazingly intense discussions, mainly because we were so different and opinionated. Chris has a pixie face, bright blue eyes, and wispy sand-colored hair, which makes her seem as light as the froth on an ice-cream soda. But the minute she opens her mouth, that impression dissolves, for she has a surprisingly deep voice, and anything but a frothy mentality. She is co-captain of the debating team, which is unusual for a tenth-grader.

Bambi is probably the most inappropriately named person in the world. Even she makes fun of her name and says that "Dumbo" or "Thunder-Thighs" would be more suitable. Of course the reason she can make fun of herself is because she's so good looking: long thick chestnut hair, dark green eyes, and a flawless complexion that even in mid-winter seems to have a tan.

I was busy evenly apportioning our double order of

French fries while Chris was telling us about her oldest sister, Molly, who was already in college.

"My parents are ecstatic because Molly has been accepted in some special program in early childhood development. There's actually a nursery school on campus where she gets to work with the kids and make observations that she can use for her thesis. Personally, I don't see anything so great about working with other people's children."

"I'm with you," Bambi agreed. "If they're not your own, forget it."

"I don't feel that way," Nina said. "I love little kids. I think I'll want to specialize in pediatrics."

"I can't think of anything worse than taking care of somebody else's child." Chris munched thoughtfully on a French fry.

"You already said that," I snapped.

"That's because I believe it. I gather you don't?"

"I think you have a very narrow view. What's wrong with loving someone else's kid?" It was hard for me not to sound petulant.

"Nothing's wrong with it. It just isn't for me."

"I think that shows how really selfish you are." The minute that slipped out I regretted it, and I could feel my cheeks burn with embarrassment. Seeing three sets of eyes looking at me as though I'd flipped out didn't help matters.

"I don't think Sally meant that," Nina said, trying to rescue me.

"I didn't, Chris," I mumbled.

"I certainly hope not. We're having a perfectly normal discussion and you start getting personal." Chris was indignant, and I didn't blame her.

"I really am sorry, Chris. I don't think you're selfish at all," I apologized.

19

"Let's forget it, Sally," Chris said, but she still had a puzzled look on her face.

Then Bambi changed the subject completely and told us her experience of trying out for the role of Nettie Fowler in *Carousel*, the musical the school was presenting in the spring. Bambi has a talent for embellishing stories about herself but she never sounds conceited. That's probably because although she's the heroine, she always makes fun of herself.

As she was describing the tryout, I was only half listening because I was still upset about attacking Chris. Nina and Chris were making comments and giggling while Bambi built up the story.

"I know I'm the best-qualified person for the part," she explained, "but the odds are against me."

"Why?" Nina asked.

"Because the role of Mr. Snow has already been chosen, and in the tryout I had to sing this romantic duet with him."

"So?" the others asked in unison.

"When I got up to sing, the rest of the cast, including Mr. Owen, the director, started to laugh. That made me feel very self-conscious for a minute, but then I cracked up too, because Charlie Berman was Mr. Snow, and if I got down on my knees I think I'd still be a head taller than he."

"Did you actually sing?" Chris asked.

"We finally pulled ourselves together, and although I knew we were an absurd couple, our voices blended perfectly. The problem was that even with Charlie standing on his tippie-toes, we weren't eye level. I felt like the *Queen Elizabeth II* being accompanied by a tugboat."

Nina and Chris collapsed in laughter, but I just couldn't get into it. I hoped no one noticed, but later, when we were walking home, Nina must have observed what a downer I was having. Bambi and Chris were ahead of us, and Nina whispered, "You didn't say anything that bad, and Chris has probably already forgotten about it."

"Hope so," I muttered.

"Then what are you worrying about?"

"Not sure," I said, but I already knew that something a lot deeper than my sniping at Chris would account for my bad mood. And I couldn't shake it, even though I should have been looking forward to a terrific evening. That night Eric and I were going to the new Monty Python movie with Eric's best friend, Bobby, and his most recent girlfriend, nicknamed Cookie.

Bobby is a tall, freckle-faced redhead with a perpetual twinkle in his eye. He and Eric are the star doubles players on the tennis team, and that's the only time Bobby is ever serious about anything. His romance with Cookie has lasted a record five weeks, and I've gotten to know her even though she's a year ahead of me. Unlike a lot of eleventh-grade girls, she's not the least bit snobby. If anything, she's suspiciously sweet, and with her blond cherubic looks, she reminds me of spun sugar.

I managed to stay absorbed in the movie, but afterwards, when we were sitting at a table at the Fount, the ice-cream parlor next to the theater, I found myself interrupting everything that was said in terms of what I was beginning to think of as my problem. Even the most innocent conversation bothered me.

Bobby and Eric were complimenting themselves on the tennis match they had just won against the number-two-seeded doubles players of a nearby school.

"Thanks to you, Bobby, we won the tie breaker. Your serve was really on."

"It's your speed that did it," Bobby insisted. "You were running around that court like a gazelle."

"I can thank my father for that," Eric remarked.

"Your father?" I piped up. "What's he got to do with it?"

"He was a track star at college, and I think I inherited his legs."

"Genes are important," I said gloomily.

" 'Fraid so," Cookie interjected. "You see, I always wanted dark brown eyes like yours, Sally, but there was no way, not with two blue-eyed parents."

"Can't we talk about something else?" I barked. "I can't stand these scientific discussions."

They looked at me in amazement, because I rarely sounded so contentious. I realized that for the second time that day I had over-reacted to a perfectly normal discussion.

"You're the one that mentioned genes," Eric observed. I could tell he was annoyed.

"Look," Bobby said, "if we don't get into Mendel's theory of heredity a little more deeply than this, I don't think you can accuse us of having a heavy sci session, Sally." He was trying to keep things light.

"Right," Cookie agreed. "I've never been accused of being scientific, but I wish you'd tell old Gruber about it. Then maybe he'd stop giving me Z's in biology." Was she being saccharine sweet or subtly sarcastic? Whichever, there wasn't much I could say.

The rest of the evening, I was unusually quiet. Although I'd objected to the conversation about heredity, I was anxious to get home and read up on it. Maybe I'd find something that would suggest that environment was more important. But if that were the case, my environment might have been something else entirely. I might have been adopted by a Hollywood movie mogul—they were always adopting children—or been raised by a missionary in China. There were all sorts of exotic possibilities.

These thoughts whirled around in my head, and I hardly noticed that I hadn't participated in the conversation until I was alone with Eric. We had dropped off Bobby and Cookie, and Eric had pulled up his red Rabbit to the front of my house. I started to open the car door, but Eric put his arm on my shoulder.

"What's bugging you, Sal?" he asked softly. "You're not yourself."

"Maybe that's the problem."

"What do you mean?"

"I don't know," I said, still uptight and not wanting to talk about it.

"Look, lambchop," he said, pulling me close to him, "whenever you do want to talk, I'm here."

"I know," I said, grateful that he wasn't chewing me out for being such a deadhead all night.

"I love you, Sal," he whispered, and gently pressed my head against his shoulder. Ordinarily, he would have begun kissing me, but he sensed that I just wanted to be held. For the longest time we stayed there while he stroked my hair and I clung to him.

When we finally separated and he walked me up the path to my house, I felt a lot calmer.

"Remember, you can always count on me," he said, as I slipped quietly into the house.

"I know, I know," I told him, "and I don't want to spoil it."

Before he could ask any more questions, I closed the door and ran upstairs to my room. Then, for the first time in ages, I sank down on my bed and the tears uncontrollably rolled down my face. After a few minutes, I got ready for bed, splashed cold water on my face, and felt more in control. But much as I wanted to, I could not turn off my mind.

I grabbed my biology book off the shelf and turned to the chapter on genes. My eye immediately caught the line: "The form of each new individual is determined, aside from environmental shaping, by the genes inherited from the parents." I already knew that was true, but seeing that statement in black and white only reinforced my need to know more about myself.

I climbed into bed and tried to fall asleep, but there were so many unanswered questions and what-might-have-beens. Who were my natural parents? What would my life have been like if they had kept me—at least one of them? If I hadn't been adopted, might I have been raised in an orphanage? What would have happened if I'd been adopted by another family, or perhaps a single person? Questions, questions, questions.

It must have been well after two in the morning before I fell into an exhausted sleep.

Chapter 4.

For the next few weeks I made a superhuman effort to appear normal. I went out of my way to be cheerful and friendly, and on at least six different occasions I bit my tongue before making a crack that would reveal what was uppermost on my mind. But I've never been good at deception, and keeping up the pretense of being happy when I was in a constant state of turmoil was almost impossible. I naively hoped that some external event would restore my equilibrium. I was waiting, waiting for that magical moment.

Meanwhile, I concentrated on my photography, an interest that in the past I had found totally absorbing. I was preparing a group of photos tentatively called "A Park for All Seasons," which was to become part of the school's end-of-the-year photography exhibit. My purpose was to show that the park in our neighborhood, with its swings, slides, sprinkler, and sandbox surrounded by maple trees, had a distinct personality determined by the time of the year. In the sweltering summer I'd snapped kids shrieking with delight while they ran in and out of a sprinkler. In the autumn, I focused on the spectacular colors of the leaves, which ranged from deep red to burnished copper and amber.

I still had winter and spring to do, and although it was Sunday, a few weeks before winter began officially on December 21, I thought I'd get a head start. The trees had already shed their leaves and were a perfect subject for winter. Later I would photograph some snow scenes.

It was a gray morning—light enough for me to take pictures without a flash, but wintry in feeling. The park would be in contrast to my summer and fall prints. After I was done with my photography session, I was going to Eric's house for brunch. He likes to sleep late on Sunday, and I don't mind being alone when I'm taking pictures.

The park was deserted except for a couple of daddies who were pushing their little kids on the swings. The temperature was in the thirties, and the kids were bundled up to the eyeballs in jackets and scarves and hats. I took a couple of candids of them, and then worked on the starkness of the bare trees. I had used up a whole roll of film, and sat down on a bench in front of an empty sandbox in order to reload my camera. I was so involved in what I was doing that I sensed, rather than saw, that someone had sat down beside me. I didn't bother to look up until I'd clicked the camera shut.

"Eric!" I screamed. "How long have you been here?"

"A few minutes," he said, "but I didn't want to scare you and have you mess up your film."

"Is something wrong?" I asked. He looked troubled.

"Not exactly."

"But something must be the matter. Why else would you be out on this frigid Sunday morning?"

"I wanted to talk to you before you came to the house."

"Stop being so mysterious." I was getting impatient.

"It has to do with Christmas vacation."

"What about it?"

"I'm going to Palm Beach over the holidays."

"You're what?" It wasn't easy for me to take in what he was saying, because we'd already planned so many things, not the least of which was a progressive New Year's Eve party, starting with punch and hors d'oeuvres at my house and ending with punch and dessert at his.

"It's my grandmother's seventy-fifth birthday and this is a command performance. My grandfather is actually putting us up at a hotel because their apartment isn't big enough for all of us. He says it's the best present he could give her."

"And the worst he could give me," I muttered.

"Sal, you know I'd love to invite you, but that's impossible. Then my kid brother and sister would want to bring a friend, and seeing as we're staying at a hotel, we can't take along any extras."

"How come you didn't tell me sooner, so I could make some other plans?" I wanted to get back at him, but the truth was there were no other plans I could make.

"I didn't know for sure until this morning. My grandmother called and said the reservations were confirmed. My mother told Janie, and she was so excited she came bounding into my room to tell me. I knew that's all we'd be talking about at brunch, so I thought I'd better warn you."

I could just imagine Janie, Eric's ten-year-old sister who's a nonstop talker, prattling on with her thirteen-year-old brother, Scott, about the sailing and snorkeling and swimming they'd be into in a couple of weeks.

"Thanks a lot for warning me," I said tonelessly. "You're really thoughtful."

"Honest, Sally, I'd rather be here with you over the holidays, but I can't disappoint my family."

"I know," I sighed resignedly. "It's not your fault." I wanted to be a good sport, although I felt abandoned.

"Do you want to take some more pictures?" Eric asked, indicating there wasn't much more for either of us to say about his news.

"I'm not feeling too creative now."

"Then let's go back to my house. It's almost time for brunch anyway, and you know how Ingrid is if we're late for her pancakes."

Ingrid was the Swedish cook who had been with the family ever since Eric was born. She was plump and jolly except when it came to meals, and then she ruled with an iron hand. She once told me and Eric that if she had her way, everybody would be seated at the table at least ten minutes before food was served; that way she could guarantee the correct temperature.

There was more formality at Eric's house than I was accustomed to. Mr. Lawrence, a straightforward, slightly graying man who had the build of a former athlete, always wore a jacket at the dining room table. And Mrs. Lawrence, a petite, delicate-faced woman who wore her hair in a French twist, was always elegantly dressed—long gowns at dinner, frocks probably made in France at lunch, and perfectly tailored custom-made slacks and silk shirts for brunch.

I wasn't usually particularly aware of the contrast in life-styles between my family and Eric's, but that day it hit me the minute I entered the house. It looked like a scene out of a Victorian novel: in the antique-furnished, pine-paneled den Mr. and Mrs. Lawrence seated on matching chintz chairs sipping Bloody Marys beside a roaring fire, while Janie and Scott played Monopoly on a gaming table that was permanently set up in the corner of the room, with Brassy, their golden retriever, at their feet.

In my house, my blue-jeaned father would be working on the Sunday crossword puzzle, his scruffy boots resting on the slate-topped coffee table he had built himself; my mother, wearing her old gray flannel skirt and black turtleneck, which had seen better days, would be poring over the real estate section; and my cat, Peaches, would probably be nestling in the corner of the couch, where there were always traces of her hair.

The Lawrences were very hospitable, and Janie especially seemed to love it when I came over. She always had something special to show me. Once, when she dragged me into her room to see four new dresses that her mother had bought for her in Italy and I was genuinely enthusiastic at how beautiful they were, she confided to me that she wished I was her sister. I knew she was sincere, and even though Eric and I agreed she was spoiled rotten, it was hard not to like Janie. Besides being the youngest, she was adorable looking: a mop of black curly hair, a snub nose, enormous dark eyes, and that enchanting smile that seemed to run in the family.

As soon as Janie saw me enter the room, she slipped off her chair, said to Scott, "To be continued," and ran up to me, babbling a mile a minute.

"We're going to Florida," she screeched, "for ten whole days. Isn't that terrific? It's Granny's birthday and Gramps is giving her *us* for a present—for ten days, anyway—and Mommy says I can get a new bathing suit, maybe a bikini. I can't imagine Christmas without snow, but it'll be worth it if I can go swimming and everything, don't you think, Sally?"

"Janie, give Sally a chance to catch her breath," Mrs. Lawrence told her. Then she turned to me. "Hello, dear."

"How are you, Sally?" Mr. Lawrence greeted me.

"Fine," I lied, looking down at my camera, which I was still holding.

"See you've been taking some pictures," Scott observed. Scott was usually painfully shy, according to Eric, and the fact that he ever spoke to me was a sign that I made it with all the Lawrences. Scott looked like his mother—the same fine chiseled features—and I kidded Eric that his kid brother would definitely be the Casanova in the family.

Then Ingrid appeared at the entrance to the den, arms akimbo, and announced that brunch would be ready in exactly twelve minutes. Before she backed away, she smiled at me and said, "I can count on you to be on time, Sally."

"I'd never be late for your pancakes," I said, feigning a cheerfulness I certainly didn't feel, and smiling at her. I turned back and added, "I'd better wash up and leave my camera in the hall so I don't forget it."

As I left the room, I heard Janie saying, "Scott, don't forget to take *your* camera to Palm Beach. I want to make sure you get some pictures of me water-skiing. Nobody in my class believes I can get up on them, and this would be proof. Carol and Muffy think they're the only ones . . ."

I parked my camera on the marble table in the foyer and, gritting my teeth, went into the powder room. I slowly washed my hands, wondering how I would get through the next couple of hours. I tried to replace my grim reflection in the mirror with a smile, but it looked more like a grimace. Relax, I told myself, it's only ten days. I can survive—I hope. I took several deep breaths, as though I were preparing for a marathon, and briskly returned to the den.

Janie's enthusiasm was irrepressible, and while the rest of us pigged out on pancakes and syrup, she asked a lot of questions, none of which required an answer: "Should I bring back shells for my friends, or just postcards? Will Granny have seventy-six candles on her cake—one to grow on? It'll have to be a huge cake. Do you suppose Granny and Gramps are too old to swim?"

Finally, Mr. Lawrence suggested that she quiet down and someone else be allowed to speak. He asked me about what kind of pictures I'd been taking, and I told him about my project. Scott wanted to know if I only used color 35-milimeter film, or black and white.

"Color, I bet," Janie assumed correctly.

"You're right," I told her.

"Sounds terrific," Janie approved.

"They are," Eric assured her. "Very professional."

"I'd love to see them," Mrs. Lawrence said. "I hope you'll bring them over one day."

"I will," I promised, and basked in all the attention.

But then Janie cried, "You've given me a great idea, Sally. My dumb homeroom teacher says she wants us to keep a journal or paint a picture or something about our Christmas vacation. She says she doesn't want our mind to go blank over the holidays and if we *exercise* it, it won't. I was trying to think of something easy and I think I'll take pictures with my Polaroid, which doesn't take such good pictures, but so what, she won't know the difference. I'll call it 'Christmas in the Sun.' Do you mind if I steal your idea?"

"Course not," I said.

"Imitation is the highest form of flattery," Mrs. Lawrence remarked.

Then, inevitably, the conversation turned back to the Lawrences' vacation and what would be the best kind of pictures to represent a tropical Christmas—Santa Claus in a bathing suit or a palm tree strung with Christmas-tree lights. By the time we were finished with our dessert of fruit compote and lace cookies, I was back in a blue downer.

Eric walked me home, apologizing all the way about Janie's insistence on talking about herself and her vacation.

"Can't blame her," I said perversely. "If I were going to Florida, I'd talk about it too."

That put a damper on the conversation, and when we got to my door, I mumbled something about having to practice the violin.

"I'd invite you in, but I really have to practice," I explained.

"I know," he said. "Sunday is your music and photography day."

It was true, but I think Eric and I both knew I needed an excuse to be by myself.

"See ya, lambchop," he said, and gently squeezed my hand.

"See ya," I said, and let myself into the house.

As I hung up my coat, I knew I was being unreasonable. I knew Eric didn't want to go away, he'd rather be with me, and he didn't care a fig about a tropical vacation. But still I felt deserted.

Chapter 5.

I wasn't ready to tell Lucy and George about my disappointment over Christmas vacation, but I was mad at the world. I couldn't help thinking that the external event I was hoping for to restore my equilibrium seemed less and less likely to occur. In fact, just the opposite was happening, with Eric telling me his news.

My parents had set up a card table in the living room and were playing bridge with our neighbors, the Manfelds. Irene Manfeld is very friendly and enthusiastic, compared to her reserved husband, Albert. They are childless and always make a big fuss over me, so although I wasn't in the mood for socializing, I knew they'd be insulted if I didn't say hello. I forced myself to smile, and went in.

Irene was shuffling the cards and scolding her husband for not leading back a spade, when she saw me.

"Sally, darling, I hoped we'd catch you. How are you?"

I exchanged greetings with everyone and gave Irene and Albert a peck on the cheek.

"Pull up a chair and bring me some luck," Albert urged.

"Have to practice, but I'll see you later," I said, backing out of the room and waving.

When I was climbing the stairs I heard Irene say, "She is such a doll!"

"Don't I know it!" Lucy agreed.

"We always say how lucky we are," George added.

Hearing those words made me feel worse than ever, guilty as well as forlorn, for in some way I blamed them for what happened to me. It wasn't their fault that Eric was being dragged away from me, but why couldn't it have been the other way: *me* leaving *him*. At least then I would have something to look forward to—sunny beaches instead of gray weather, even though we were apart.

I closed the door to my room, set up my music stand, and began working on the second violin's part in Beethoven's First Symphony, which the school orchestra was doing for our winter concert. Usually I enjoy practicing, but nothing went right. My bowing arm felt stiff and my fingering was off so that the notes weren't on pitch. I was sure my violin problems were reflecting my mood, and I was determined to overcome them by warming up with some scales. Scales are boring, but I knew they would help get me back on the track, so I put aside the Beethoven and sawed away.

I hadn't worked on the scales for more than three minutes when the E string broke. I was totally demoralized, and although I had an extra string, I was too disheartened to bother changing it. I shoved the violin and bow back in the case, and then gazed out the window, vaguely wondering what I should do.

It was only three-thirty and I had the rest of the afternoon to kill. Ordinarily I would have relished a free afternoon, since there were a zillion projects I could pursue. For one thing, I had started knitting a six-foot-long scarf for Eric for Christmas—each foot was to be a different color—and I'd only finished two feet. But now it didn't seem like a very appropriate gift. I thought bitterly that maybe I could convert the two feet I'd completed into a pair of swimming trunks. Also, I was in the middle of *Jane Eyre* and loving it, but I was too restless to settle down and read. I thought maybe I should go downstairs and whip up some butterscotch cookies, the one culinary endeavor in which I excelled, but that suddenly seemed like more work than fun.

If only there were some excitement in my life, something new and different to get me out of the doldrums. I decided I'd better call Nina, who's always practical without being judgmental and invariably makes me feel better. I went into my parent's room, flopped on their queen-size bed, and dialed her number. The line was busy, and I didn't get through to her for ten minutes.

"I was just about to call you," she said. She sounded unusually excited and I was sure she had some special news to tell me. "I've been talking to Rosie."

Rosie was Nina's cousin, the same age as us, and lived in a twelve-room co-op in Manhattan overlooking Central Park. Rosie went to an elite girls' school in the city and was very sophisticated. She was tall and carried herself like a princess, and had a mane of black hair that she tossed dramatically whenever she spoke. I personally thought she was a super-snob, but Nina defended her, saying she was covering up a feeling of insecurity. Rosie was in the shadow of her older sister, Andrea, who had graduated from the same school and walked off with all the honors. Andrea was the brain of the family, and even though Rosie was the beauty, Rosie felt inferior, according to Nina. Nina claimed that once Rosie knew you liked her, she shed all her affectations, and the problem was that I just didn't know her well enough. If I was honest, I knew I was a little jealous of their relationship, because even though Nina and I were best friends, Rosie was her cousin. Blood is thicker than water, as the saying goes.

"What did Rosie want?" I asked.

"Well, it's good news for me, but I'm afraid you won't like it."

"Why?" I couldn't imagine what she was about to tell me.

"She's invited me to go skiing with her and her family in Aspen over the holidays. They've rented a chalet for the whole vacation and she's allowed to bring a friend. The reason she chose me was because she didn't want to offend any of her friends at school, and since I'm her cousin . . ."

"And you're going, of course." I couldn't help my sarcastic tone.

"I hate to mess up our plans about New Year's Eve and everything, but you know how much I love skiing. Also, her mother checked with my folks to make sure it was all right before she asked me, and they said it was okay, that the trip would be my main present, and I'd have to hold off on getting a new guitar and—"

"I don't really blame you," I interrupted resignedly.

"You'll have Eric to keep you busy, anyway."

"No, I won't."

"What do you mean?"

"Eric's going to Palm Beach with his family."

"Sally, you're kidding!"

"I wish I were."

"But that's awful! Maybe I should get out of going to Aspen, then."

"Don't be ridiculous. That would make me feel even worse."

"But you're my best friend, and I don't want that to change, ever."

"And you're my best friend, so I wouldn't want you to give up a skiing vacation just to keep me entertained. No reason for us both to be miserable." I tried to laugh, but it didn't come off.

"There'll still be plenty of kids here, and who knows, maybe you'll have an unexpected adventure."

"Sure, I'll probably break my leg skating at Kelton's." Kelton's was the local indoor ice-skating rink, where I'd been going ever since I could remember.

"At least you haven't lost your sense of humor."

"I wasn't being funny. At this point a broken leg doesn't seem so terrible, compared to my other problems."

"I know, Sal. I just wish I could say or do something to cheer you up."

"I'll be okay. It's only a couple of weeks out of my life."

"Right! And Chris and Bambi will be around."

"Unless they've been invited by Charles and Di to spend Christmas at Sandringham."

Nina laughed. "You do have a lively imagination."

"That's all that's left," I answered gloomily.

Then I heard Nina's twelve-year-old sister, Nancy, shouting in the background. "Hurry up, Nina. You've been on the phone for ten hours and you promised you'd help me with my vocabulary."

"Hear that?" Nina asked me. "The penalty of being a good sister. I did promise I'd help her, though, so I better hang up."

"I understand," I muttered, thinking that, for whatever reason, I seemed to be at the bottom of everyone's priority list.

"See you tomorrow, Sal. And feel better."

"I'll try," I said, and slowly put down the receiver.

But feeling better didn't seem in the realm of possibility with Eric surfing in the balmy South, Nina skiing in the spectacular West, and me stuck in the boring borough of the Bronx.

I was quiet all through supper, unwilling to initiate any conversations and responding in monosyllables to direct questions. My bad mood hovered over the dining room table like an impenetrable thick cloud, and finally Lucy and George tactfully ignored me and rehashed their bridge hands. George admonished Lucy for jumping to slam without asking for aces through the Blackwood convention.

"But dear, if I have a hundred honors six times in one suit and an outside ace, why not take the risk?"

"Because two aces are missing, and you'll be down one."

The whole conversation was excruciatingly boring but allowed me to wallow in my pool of despondency. Dullsville, I thought; bridge, life, everything. Unaware that I was speaking out loud, I mumbled under my breath, "Boring, boring, boring."

"What did you say, Sal?" my mother asked.

"I said, why don't we ever go anyplace?"

My father looked at me in surprise, and then smiled.

"We do, every summer for three weeks, to the Adirondacks, remember?"

"That's not what I mean," I growled.

"You mean someplace exotic like the West Indies," Lucy offered.

"Or Florida or out West. Anything but the same old thing, every single vacation. We never do anything different."

"As a matter of fact, Sally, I was going to surprise you, but now seems as good a time as any to tell you. Willie Brown, in my office, has offered me his box at Madison Square Garden for any time I want in December to see the ice show. I think there are about six seats, and you can invite some friends to join us."

"Terrific," I muttered.

Now it was Lucy's turn to register surprise. "I thought you loved the ice show! Last year tickets were at a premium so we didn't bother to get them, but now that we can have them free, you don't seem to be interested."

"You just don't understand."

"What don't we understand?" George was no longer in a bantering mood. "Mother was thrilled that she got the seats, and not just for us but for your friends, too."

"My friends won't be here."

"Won't be here?"

"Eric's going to Palm Beach, and Nina's going to Aspen, and the only place I get to go is the ice show!"

With that I pushed back my chair and bolted upstairs before I burst into tears. Now they knew what was bothering me, but I didn't want them to see me cry. Normally, I would rely on Lucy and George to see me through all the crises in my life, but I knew the only person who could see me through this one was me.

Chapter 6.

After that scene, there was an imperceptible change in my relationship with my parents. I knew I was responsible and that they couldn't help reacting to a distance I had created between us. The problem was, I couldn't help myself. George, as always, tried to kid with me. The next day at breakfast he was glancing at the paper and read aloud an ad for a ten-day tour of Switzerland that only cost $1500 and that he might send me on over Christmas and New Year's. I didn't find that particularly funny, and couldn't even bring myself to smile. Then I noticed Lucy frowning at him and quickly begin talking about the busy day she had scheduled.

"I have three different clients who have to be shown half a dozen houses. I have to arrange to get the keys or make sure the owners are home. It's great being busy, but I am looking forward to the office being closed for a week between Christmas and New Year's."

"Is that all we can talk about?" I asked angrily.

"Sally, I was talking about my job, not the holidays. In fact, I was trying—unsuccessfully, I guess—to get your father off the subject."

"I suppose," I grumbled.

"Listen, Miss Grumps, I want you to put your present mood on hold, because as soon as vacation begins, I want to enlist your help in sanding down this dining room table. It's got more potholes than any side street in New York, and you can take out all your aggression on it."

"Oh, Daddy, sometimes you don't understand anything," I whined, and for the second time in less than twenty-four hours I had to rush out of the room before the tears spilled down my face.

"What on earth did I say wrong?" I heard George ask as I climbed the stairs.

"I wish I knew," my mother answered. "Something tells me her reaction has to do with more than Nina and Eric leaving town."

"I've always prided myself that she was amazingly content to do things with me. Remember last spring when she helped refinish that old chest of drawers that we picked up at the flea market? She couldn't wait to work on it every spare minute."

"I know, George, but now she couldn't care less about helping you with the dining room table."

"She's right about one thing, though! Sometimes I just don't understand anything."

It made me feel worse than ever, knowing I'd hurt George's feelings. Naturally, we'd had our share of squabbles in the past, but he always made light of them, and the only time he really got mad at me was when I did something that he thought might be dangerous. Like the time I was about eleven years old and I decided to show a couple of boys—the Graber kids, who had just moved into a house down the block—how to use my father's electric saw. My parents had gone shopping for groceries one Saturday morning and told me they'd be gone about an hour and that I should "mind the fort." Tony and Andy Graber happened to drop over shortly after they left, and I was eager to impress these two exceedingly handsome "older" new guys in town. Tony was almost twelve and Andy was thirteen, and they couldn't believe that I could operate an electric saw. I wasn't sure I could either, but I'd seen my father use it and it seemed very simple.

I dragged the saw out of the shed in the backyard and attached the cord to an extension outlet in the kitchen. Then Tony and Andy manfully carried an oversized log from the cord of wood piled in the shed for me to work on. I was all set to go when George appeared, his arms loaded with bundles of groceries, and screamed, "Stop that!" Simultaneously he dropped the groceries. Oranges rolled around like billiard balls, eggs leaked out of their cardboard carton, and soda bottles crashed to smithereens.

I dropped the saw and leapt away from it as though I'd been struck by lightning. It was the first time George had ever screamed at me. Tony and Andy were momentarily awestruck, but then Lucy, who had parked the car in front of the house and was oblivious to what was going on, took in the scene from the kitchen window and calmly suggested that we all pitch in and salvage what we could. My father, looking ashen, sank down on the back step while Tom and Andy picked up the groceries and brought them into the kitchen. They were very polite, and Lucy thanked them profusely and invited them to stay for lunch. But they were eager to get away, and explained that they had promised to clean up *their* yard. "I don't think our folks will appreciate it if they find us working on someone else's,'' Andy said.

Neither of them seemed to have too much of a sense of humor, and when they hurried off, I decided I'd better find a better way to make an impression.

Later my father apologized for overreacting, and mumbled something about how it was possible to love someone too much.

''It is if you stop a person from doing her thing,'' Lucy remarked.

''Unless her thing involves doing irreparable damage,'' George countered.

I recalled that whole incident now as I splashed water on my face and blotted it dry. It was a cameo of how we reacted to each other. My father's loving protectiveness, my mother's more reasonable calm, me wanting to assert my independence. The difference was that then I wasn't even a teenager, but now I was practically grown-up. I guess our positions had hardened—mine, anyway. I wasn't sure what I wanted, but I knew it had to do with what Lucy had called ''doing her thing.''

I applied a tiny bit of powder on my nose in order to cover the telltale signs of crying, blush-on and lip gloss so I didn't look so pale, and then vigorously brushed my hair. At least I looked normal, even though I didn't feel it. Then I made my bed, and took my time stuffing my books and pencils into my canvas bag so that I could hurry out of the house without getting into another discussion with my parents.

They were still at the dining room table as I rushed by them and yelled good-bye. I wanted to get away without any further confrontation.

I'm not sure how I got through the next couple of weeks. Naturally, everyone was talking about the Christmas holidays, but Eric and I pretended they weren't happening. That actually made things worse—like ignoring an elephant in your living room.

The school concert took place the night before vacation began. In addition to the orchestra playing Beethoven, the madrigal group, according to tradition, sang Christmas carols. It was a time of high excitement and emotion. I could feel myself choking up, and it took all my willpower not to weep in public. I would have felt like a complete idiot, since I was the second violin and all the orchestra members as well as the audience would have seen this stupid display.

After the concert there was a reception in the gym where all the parents oohed and ahhed over our performance. I put on my frozen smile and pretended to be enjoying myself. If Lucy and George saw through me, they didn't let on. The crowd of parents dwindled, and a lot of the kids headed for Roger's house. Roger was the percussionist, a round, jolly type, who exalted in beating the drums and clashing the symbols and for the last three years had thrown a party for the Friends of the Orchestra and Madrigal Group.

Of course Eric and I had planned to go together, and as we drove over, he expounded all the way on how great the orchestra sounded, especially the string section. I didn't feel like talking, and even if I had, there wouldn't have been the opportunity. I think he was afraid of there being a silence between us, or of what I might say.

Roger lived in a humungus Victorian house on an old Riverdale estate. The party was going strong in the downstairs rec room, which was equipped with a standing bar and Japanese lanterns and decorated for the occasion with balloons, Christmas lights, holly, and mistletoe. Rock music blared out of the speakers located at opposite ends of the room, and as we came down the stairs, I could feel the ebullience. This was always one of the best parties, probably because it was a prelude to our vacation and for the next couple of weeks we had nothing but a good time to look forward to. In the past, that's how I'd felt, too.

We headed for the bar, and Roger, who was playing bartender, served us some sodas.

"Hey, smile, Sally. You look like you lost your last friend," Roger teased.

"In a way that's true," I mumbled, but Roger was already filling someone else's glass and wasn't listening.

We leaned against the bar and sipped our drinks in silence. There was too much noise to carry on a normal conversation, so Eric didn't bother to try.

"Want to dance?" he asked after about five minutes of people-watching.

"Why not?" I replied without enthusiasm.

We put our glasses on the bar and edged our way through the crowd to the center of the floor, which had been blocked out for dancing. The dim light, which some might have considered romantic, made it very hard for me to see. I was unavoidably jostled by the dancers who were leaping around to an energetic punk tape, and as I was trying to keep up with Eric, who was running interference for me, someone crashed down on my foot. I let out a blood-curdling scream that was drowned out by the music, and hobbled off the floor. Eric looked back to see what had happened, and rushed over to where I had slumped into a chair against the wall.

"You okay?" he asked solicitously. "What happened?"

"Some gorilla landed on my foot," I explained, taking off my shoe and pointing to my instep, which had developed a black and blue egg.

"I'll get you some ice. That'll make the swelling go down."

He rushed off while I stared in fascination at the bump on my foot, which now felt numb. Eric was back in a flash with ice cubes wrapped in a towel, and knelt down in front of me.

"At your service, madam," he said.

"Thanks," I groaned.

"You'll do anything to get out of dancing with me." He was trying to chat me up, but the numbness was wearing off and I felt grimmer than ever.

"We might as well leave, before you have to carry me out."

"There's nothing I'd like better than to carry you." Eric's smile could have melted the ice cubes, but I couldn't respond.

"I'm serious, Eric. You'd better take me home."

"Okay, okay. I'll explain the situation to Roger and we'll split."

"Don't make a scene," I instructed. "What I don't want now is a lot of kids gaping at me."

"Whatever you say, Sal," he agreed, taking the ice pack off my foot.

He pulled me to a standing position, wrapped my arm around his neck, and, holding my waist, helped me hop to the stairs. With half my weight leaning on him, I limped to the car.

When we arrived at my house, I went into my hopping act. My parents had already gone upstairs to bed, so we had the living room to ourselves. Since we were rarely alone, except in his car, this should have been a bonus, but under the circumstances it didn't make much difference where we were. Eric had seated himself beside me on the couch, his arm around my shoulder, but my foot was killing me and I wasn't even tempted to hold hands. He leaned over to kiss me and accidentally brushed my sore foot with his loafer.

"Ouch!" I yelped.

He immediately realized what had happened and leapt back as though he'd received an electric shock. "I just wanted to kiss you good-bye," he apologized.

"I know, Eric, but you'd better go. My foot really hurts, and you've got to catch a plane tomorrow morning. I bet you probably haven't packed yet."

"I hate to leave you like this. Maybe you should see a doctor."

"It's just a dumb bruise. I'll give it an aspirin tonight and probably by tomorrow it will be fine."

"Will the rest of you be fine, too?" I could see he was genuinely concerned.

"Why not?" I asked, trying to keep my lip from trembling and mad at myself for behaving like a wimp.

"You know I'll miss you, Sally, and I'll be thinking of you every minute."

"I know," I whispered. "Same here."

He held my face in his hands and then closed his lips over mine. For the moment, at least, I forgot all about pain.

Chapter 7.

The pain in my foot subsided, but the rest of me—my head—didn't improve. The swelling on my instep continued, and I had to wear a loosely laced sneaker for the next two weeks, which meant I couldn't go sleigh-riding or ice skating. There were still plenty of things to do—more parties, movies, Christmas shopping, as well as my projects around the house. I helped George with the dining room table and worked on Eric's scarf—we'd decided to exchange presents when he returned—but my heart wasn't in any of these activities. It was the first time in my life that Christmas vacation was a total and complete bummer.

I knew it wasn't fair, but I couldn't suppress my growing resentment toward Lucy and George. I'd always been proud of the fact that George was a schoolteacher, and that Lucy couldn't have cared less about material things, but suddenly it seemed everyone had more advantages than I had. Again, I was nagged by wanting to know where I came from, who I was, what might have been. My feeling of being different from my family was intensifying, and my sense of alienation peaked on New Year's Day.

I had not quite recovered from the worst New Year's Eve of my life. Instead of a progressive party, we went to Bambi's house for an interminable evening of junk food and disco music. I was a self-made wallflower because although a number of guys asked me to dance, I didn't want to risk further damage to my injured foot, which still hurt if I didn't walk very gingerly. At the stroke of midnight, everyone had a partner to kiss but me. I missed Eric more than ever, and wondered if he could possibly feel as miserable as I did.

On New Year's Day Lucy's sister Judy, a bossy lady who loves to organize, held her annual open house, a family affair with a zillion cousins, aunts, and uncles. Judy had three boys like steps, aged eight, ten, and twelve, each born in May—the best time to have a baby, according to Judy, and proof of her highly tuned organizational ability.

I've always believed that it's a person's own responsibility to have a good time at a party. I mean you can't just be laid back and expect everyone else to entertain you. My behavior on this occasion proved my theory. Judy's kids, who usually make a big fuss over me, finally buzzed off when they saw how indifferent I was. And my Uncle Chuck, Judy's husband, who makes everything into a joke and has called me Princess for as long as I can remember, strode over to where I was slouched, sulking, on the couch and growled, "The Princess looks like she swallowed a lemon."

I've always kidded with Chuck, no matter how gross his humor, but I could barely bring myself to smile feebly.

Then he noticed my half-laced sneaker with the bump protuding on my instep, and roared, "I see you've been putting your foot in your mouth again!" He was laughing so hard I was sure he would have gone on forever if Judy hadn't yelled to him from across the room.

"We're running out of ice, Chucky, and you could do something about the fire. I think Sally can get along without you for a few minutes."

You're not kidding, I thought, and let out a sigh of relief as I watched Chuck drift off to do his wife's bidding. The rest of the afternoon I spent watching my "relatives" and feeling more and more out of it. Here I was in the bosom of my family and I felt like an alien from outer space.

There were plenty of kids who felt at odds with their families, but at least they were the same flesh and blood. They belonged to their clan, by origin if not for any other reason. More and more I wondered about my real mother. Who was she? Where did she live? Was it possible that after fifteen years she'd want to see me? I wouldn't be a burden to her now. It would ease my mind if I could meet her, see for myself where I came from. The question was how.

I was staring into the fire, so preoccupied with these thoughts that for the moment I forgot where I was, and it came as a surprise when George walked up to me, extended his hand, and announced that it was time to go.

"We're almost the last to leave," he said. "Your mother's helping Judy clear things away, and I think we should rescue her or we'll be here all night."

"Okay," I murmured distractedly as he slowly pulled me to a standing position.

On the way home I sat in the back seat of the Toyota while George and Lucy babbled on about various members of the family—how they looked or changed, how the kids had grown, and what a nice idea it was for us all to get together even though it was only once a year.

"Don't you think so, Sal?" Lucy turned to me in an obvious effort to include me in the conversation.

"Sure," I answered perfunctorily.

"I guess she doesn't think so," George remarked, half laughing.

"Personally, I think it's dumb to only get together once a year. It's so artificial." Might as well be honest.

"I don't think it's artificial," Lucy said. "After all, they're our family."

"*Your* family," I muttered, surprising even myself.

Lucy and George looked at each other as though I had uttered an obscenity, but neither of them said anything. I guess there was nothing they could say, and there was no way I could take it back. Besides, I wasn't sure I wanted to.

That remark was the dropped pebble that was to stir up what had been tranquil waters for the past fifteen years. I suppose what I'd said might be regarded as a Freudian slip. Freud claimed that sometimes people betray themselves through a slip of the tongue, and reveal what they really are thinking and feeling. This was a perfect example, because it wasn't my original intention to point out how I felt like an interloper.

The rest of the evening we all play-acted and made no reference to the bombshell I'd dropped. Since we'd pigged out at Judy's, I was spared the agony of sitting through a "polite" supper. I made a big thing about having to finish Eric's scarf; I had one foot to go and he was coming home the next day. Lucy said she had to do her real-estate homework since she hadn't bothered to look at the listings for the entire week of her vacation. And George was determined to apply a final coat of glaze to the dining room table, which was smoothed down to perfection. Since each of us was busy with our own project, we avoided getting into a serious discussion. However, there are some things that won't go away, and sooner or later I would have to talk about it.

Eric flew home the next afternoon, and less than an hour later he was on my doorstep. He threw his arms around me when I answered the door, and we hugged each other for at least five minutes in front of my house until I realized the temperature was in the teens and I was about to freeze. I pulled him into the house and slammed the door.

Lucy and George were planted in the living room in front of the fireplace. I was unreasonably annoyed with them for being there. They knew Eric and I hadn't seen each other for a million years, so why couldn't they go someplace else? Their presence didn't seem to bother Eric, who was charming as ever and, as he sat down on the hassock next to the fire, graciously answered all their questions about his vacation. It seemed Eric had come to see them, not me, when suddenly George looked at his watch and said they had to be going.

"We're having a marathon bridge session with the Manfelds, so we won't be home until after ten," Lucy said, getting up from the couch. "There's some tuna fish casserole in the fridge, Sally. You can heat it up for you and Eric."

"Okay," I said, relieved that they were finally going.

It seemed to take them forever to collect their things, but they finally got suited up in their parkas, gloves, and scarves—you would have thought they were headed for an Arctic expedition rather than a short walk down the block—and I held the door for them, as though to make sure they would actually leave. Then Eric took me in his arms and slowly kissed me. I thought that was what I wanted more than anything, but I was distracted. I hoped he didn't notice.

"I've been dreaming of this moment ever since I left you," he whispered, taking my hand and leading me to the couch.

"Me too," I said.

"But something's bothering you, Sal. You're not still mad at me, are you?"

"Why should I be? Just because you abandoned me?" I was trying to be funny, but it didn't come off.

Eric sighed hopelessly, then groped in his pocket and pulled out a small box wrapped in gold foil. "Merry Christmas, lambchop. I hope this will cheer you up."

"It will," I said brightly, "but wait. I have your present upstairs."

I dashed upstairs, and grabbed Eric's present, which I had wrapped elaborately in embossed paper and a carefully made bow.

"Wow!" he exclaimed, when I handed him the box.

We opened our presents simultaneously, and I gasped when I saw the exquisite wafer-thin locket on a thin gold chain. "Incredible," I muttered.

"You made this!" Eric shouted. "It's fantastic."

"Two great minds," I said. "We both thought of something for the neck."

"You still have your sense of humor," he laughed, slipping the locket over my head.

"Barely, Eric." I wrapped the scarf around his neck, and again he pressed his lips to mine.

"I love you, Sally," he breathed.

"I love you, too, Eric."

"Then you can tell me what's wrong. I know something

53

is bugging you and it has nothing to do with abandonment. I'm home now, with you, and I didn't want to leave you in the first place. So tell me what's wrong. It's not your foot, I hope, although I see you're still wearing a sneaker.''

"My foot is practically cured. I wish it were something that simple.''

"If it's not simple, all the more reason to talk about it.''

"You're right, I know.'' I stood up and moved purposely toward the fireplace and threw on another log. Then I sank down on the hassock, and tried to collect my thoughts. I didn't want to come across as a nerd.

As though Eric were reading my mind he said, "No matter what you say, I promise not to laugh or think you're crazy.''

"I don't know where to begin.'' I was stalling, and we both knew it.

"Why not begin at the beginning?''

"That's it!'' I exclaimed. "It's the beginning that's getting to me.''

"Meaning?''

"Meaning I don't know where I came from, or who I am, and the only way I'll find out is if I find my real parents—especially my mother. I was actually a part of her for nine months and then she gave me away. How could she do that? I have a hunch if I find her, she'll explain why, and also tell me about my father. But how can that ever happen if I don't tell Lucy and George, and they might never forgive me. They might even kick me out of the house, and then where would I be? And they've been so good to me that I wouldn't blame them, but I don't think I can go on much longer not finding out something about my past.''

I stopped long enough to catch my breath, and noticed that Eric was frowning. "Do you think I'm awful?''

"Not at all. I think you're probably very normal, and I imagine any person who's adopted would wonder about the same things."

"You'll stick by me, then, no matter what?"

"Providing it's within the law," he answered, smiling. "But for now, you owe me at least ten kisses, because that's how many nights I was away."

"Eleven, to be exact," I said, making my way toward him, and settling into the curve of his arm.

"And you complain that you're not good at math," he teased. Then we both chuckled, and although nothing had been solved, it was a great relief to have told Eric my problem and have his assurance that he was on my side.

Chapter 8.

Nina and I squealed like a couple of third-graders when we saw each other in homeroom the next day. She quickly told me that the skiing was excellent, Rosie was decent, and she had met a new guy who lived in Colorado but she didn't need a Pen Pal. I started to tell her that the best part of my vacation was yesterday when Eric came over, but we barely got started when the bell rang. I promised to go over to her house after school so we could continue.

It didn't take long for me to settle into the school routine. I think I may have been the only tenth-grader in the world who wasn't sorry to see vacation end. But it wasn't easy for me to focus on what the teacher was saying in any of my classes because I kept thinking about what I had finally expressed to Eric: I don't think I can go on much longer not finding out something about my past.

After school Nina and I chatted superficially all the way to her house, but I knew it was inevitable that I would confide in her. And once we were closeted in her room, fortified with brownies and milk, I told all. "I've got to find my real mother," I began.

"You what?" Nina, uncharacteristically, sounded shocked.

"I can't stand not knowing about her anymore, and best of all would be if I could meet her."

"What started all this?" Nina was her old thoughtful self.

"That 'Who Am I' paper got me thinking about my identity, and I thought it would end there. The next thing that happened—and I'm ashamed to admit it—was when I learned that you and Eric would be going off for the holidays. That made me wonder about who might have adopted me, and why it happened to be Lucy and George. Then everything came to a head at my aunt's party for the family. I never felt so out of it in my life."

"You believe that if you could meet your real mother, all your questions would be answered and everything would fall into place."

"Exactly!"

She didn't say anything for at least thirty seconds, and I was really afraid she'd disapprove. Therefore it was an enormous relief when she said, "I can understand what you're going through, Sally. Most kids who are adopted would feel the same way."

"That's practically what Eric said, so I guess I'm not crazy."

"Anything but. You're just facing reality."

"Something I'm not usually inclined to do." It was the first time I could laugh at myself, but my attempt to be lighthearted about my problem didn't last, and I became serious again. "I'll be haunted the rest of my life if I don't make this search."

"Then you must do it."

"Will you help me?"

"As best I can. But you've got to tell Lucy and George."

"That's going to be the toughest thing of all."

"I know, but without their support you won't find out anything."

"Maybe I can get around that by calling an adoptive tracer agency."

"You can try." Nina looked skeptical but she pulled out the Yellow Pages that she kept under her night table and began leafing through them.

"What are you looking for?"

"Here it is!" she cried. " 'Finders, Incorporated. Tracers of lost persons, specializing in adoption reunion.' "

"That's great. Where are they located?"

"Downtown Manhattan. In the West Forties, to be exact."

"That's convenient from Grand Central. I could take a train and walk over."

"You'd better call for an appointment."

"Right now?" I could feel my heart pounding faster, and I was biting my thumbnail, something I only did under enormous stress.

"If you want to go through with this, you might as well start now. And you can use my phone."

"Okay," I murmured, and slowly moved toward the phone as though I were heading for my execution.

"Courage," Nina said, jotting down the telephone number on a pad and handing it to me.

I sank down on the bed, took a deep breath, and dialed.

"Finders Inc., Tracers of Lost Persons," a woman's voice twanged. "Can I help you?"

"I want to find someone." I could barely get the words out.

"Speak up, honey. I can't hear you."

"I want to find my mother." I forced myself to speak louder.

"Your mother, you say?"

"My natural mother, that is. I'm adopted and I want to find my real mother, and your ad in the Yellow Pages says you specialize in adoption reunions." I blurted out everything fast, before I lost my nerve.

"Hold on, honey. I can make an appointment for you with one of our investigators. What's your name, and how old are you?"

"Sally Brighton. I'm fifteen."

"I'll set you up with Joey, our teenage specialist. What's the earliest you can get here after school?"

"Friday's my shortest day. I could get there by four."

"Good. And bring as much information as you can."

"Information?"

"Listen, Sally, we can't find anyone, ever, if we don't have something to go on. There're eight million people in New York and more than two hundred million in the United States. We gotta start with somethin'."

"Like what?" My mind boggled at the statistics.

"Like your real mother's name, where she lived, things about her family. You're wasting your time, and money, if you can't give us some details."

"I don't know anything," I whimpered. And I hadn't even thought about the expense.

"Well, can't you find something out?"

"I'll try," I groaned.

"Okay, kiddy. I've got you down for Friday at four."

My hand was shaking so obviously when I hung up that Nina couldn't help but notice. "You've taken a first big step," she observed.

"Yes, but I have to bring in some information so they have something to go on. And I'm going to have to pay them."

"I repeat, you can't do this without your parents' help."

"I know that, Nina, but how can I tell them?"

"You'll think of something. Now, to help you stop worrying so much, let's listen to my new Talking Heads tape. David Byrne will take your mind off your problems."

"Sure," I said without conviction, knowing full well that only an avalanche, flood, or earthquake could keep me from thinking about my quest.

That evening at supper, George went on about how pleased he was that the school administration had finally listened to him and increased the number of computers in the math department. "Makes life a lot easier for me if the kids don't have to wait in line to get their hands on one of these machines. If you learn to use the computer, Sal, your math problems will be over."

"Yep," I said, and wondered if there was a computer designed to find missing persons.

"I got a real nibble for a house that's been a white elephant for the past year." Lucy couldn't wait to tell about her day. "A family of eight is moving here from Salt Lake City, and they're desperate for a large house. The father was here checking it out today, and his wife is flying in tomorrow to decide if they'll take it."

"That's great, Lucy," George praised her. "I bet anything you're Brown and Woods' star salesperson."

"This has been a good day for both of us," Lucy said. "Me about to unload a white elephant and you finally getting your new babies."

"New babies?" I wasn't at all interested in their conversation, but that last phrase grabbed me.

George, realizing I didn't know what Lucy was referring to, couldn't miss the opportunity to tease.

"We're getting some new babies, didn't you hear?"

"What are you talking about?" My voice was edgy.

"Daddy is talking about his computer lab, Sally. Why are you so sensitive?"

"I don't know," I mumbled, and realized how silly I'd been.

I tried to think of some story I could tell about my day, like my eccentric French teacher's assignment to write a poem in French and be ready to recite and translate it in class the following week. But I just didn't feel like talking. Instead, I picked at my dish of spaghetti, explained that I'd already had brownies at Nina's, which accounted for my loss of appetite, and asked if I could be excused from the dishes because I wasn't feeling too well. It wasn't really a lie because although I wasn't physically sick, it could honestly be said I was suffering from mental anguish.

"Of course, dear," Lucy said. "I hope you're not coming down with something."

"Several kids were missing from my classes because of the flu, Sal. Now don't you go getting it." George was concerned.

"Don't worry." I didn't want to continue the subject of my health so I pushed my chair back and brought my dishes into the kitchen.

"Go lie down, Sal. We'll finish up here," Lucy advised.

"Thanks," I said, and hurried upstairs where I could brood in private.

I sat down at my desk, my unopened books piled in front of me, and wondered where I would find the courage to ask Lucy and George about my adoption. I considered writing them a letter, but that seemed cowardly and would only delay a face-to-face confrontation a brief time. Then I thought that I could call up all the adoption agencies in the area and try to glean some information. But I wasn't sure if I'd been born in New York, or if I'd been adopted through other channels, or if all records were sealed. The more I thought about it, the more desperate and frustrated I became.

I don't know how long I'd been sitting there, but the room suddenly seemed unbearably stuffy. I got up from my desk, raised the window, and took in several deep breaths of the cold night air. Although the temperature was way below freezing, my head felt clearer, and I was half-tempted to go for a walk. That was out of the question because of the "sick" act I'd pulled at supper, so I'd have to settle for sticking my head out the window.

My timing couldn't have been worse, because just at that moment there was a soft rap on my door, which I chose to ignore. Lucy, without waiting for a response and probably assuming I was fast asleep, peeked in the room.

"Sally!" she cried. "What are you doing?"

She ran toward me, pulled me back, and firmly closed the window.

"Don't look so frightened, Mother. I'm not about to leap out."

"I know, sweetie, but that's a great way to catch pneumonia, especially if you're not feeling well."

"I'm not catching anything," I protested, and sat down at my desk as though I were going to do some work.

I expected Lucy to take the hint and leave, but instead she sat down on my bed. For a few seconds the only sound in the room was of me shuffling books around. Then I purposefully opened my looseleaf notebook and uncapped my pen. Still, she didn't give any signs of leaving.

Finally, Lucy spoke softly. "What's wrong, Sally? Something's been bothering you for weeks, and I wish you'd talk about it."

"You're right," I admitted.

"Then tell me about it. You know you can trust me, and I'll do whatever I can to help."

"This time you may not." I turned to face her.

"Try me, Sal. You'd be surprised how helpful I can be." She smiled encouragingly.

This is it, now or never, I thought. "I want to find my real mother," I said as evenly as possible.

The smile disappeared from her lips, her eyes clouded. She couldn't have looked any more surprised if I had thrown a bucket of ice water at her.

"I'm sorry," I murmured. "I didn't want to tell you, and I don't blame you for hating me."

"I could never hate you, Sally, but I have to admit this was the last thing in the world I thought was troubling you. I thought maybe you were having love problems or school problems—something simple like that."

"I wish it were something simple."

"What started all this?" She still looked stricken, but the news had begun to sink in.

"I don't feel I belong anywhere." Then I told her what had triggered my thinking, and how New Year's Day I felt so out of it I might as well have been a Martian.

"We've been such a happy family," Lucy said sadly. "I never thought you were discontented."

"I wasn't, but suddenly I want to know more about me. It doesn't mean I don't love you and Daddy. I've just got to find out where I came from. I need your help."

"What kind of help?"

I explained how I'd called Finders, Inc., and made an appointment for Friday, but needed some information, and money.

Lucy shook her head in bewilderment.

"I'll pay you back one day," I promised.

"That's the least of it."

"Will you help me, Mother?"

"Please give me a chance to think. This is a lot to absorb all at once."

"I know." I sighed.

"And you'll have to tell Daddy."

"I know that, too."

Just then I heard George trudging up the stairs, and since my door was half open, it was natural for him to pop his head in my room. "Looks like a powwow," he grinned. "Don't let me interrupt."

"I think you'd better," Lucy suggested. She patted the bed, indicating he should sit down next to her.

"You two act like you're planning a war strategy." He sat down slowly.

"In a way, George. It's up to Sally to tell you."

"I don't know how to say this, Daddy," I began, trying to keep my voice from creaking.

"Just say it, Sal. We don't have any secrets."

"I—I'm looking—I want to find my real mother."

George's eyes narrowed and his body froze. I held my breath while I waited for him to say something. The silence was unbearable.

"Why?" he asked finally, his voice like steel.

"To find out who I am," I answered.

"You're Sally Brighton, that's who you are," he said, standing up and heading for the door.

"But Daddy, I have to find out more. I'm still your daughter, no matter what." I wanted desperately to reassure him.

"I'm not sure you really believe that, Sally," he said, as he turned his back on me.

Chapter 9.

The next morning George was already having coffee when I came down to breakfast. The expression on his face was grim, and there were dark circles around his eyes. He didn't look at me when I planted the customary peck on his cheek and said, "Good morning."

"Sally, I spent half the night thinking about what you told me, and I don't want you to go through with it. This search will take time and money, but far worse than that will be the emotional cost."

"I know, Daddy, but I can't help it. I can't stop thinking about who my real mother might be, and I have to look for her. If I don't succeed in finding her, at least I will have tried."

"There's no way I can talk you out of this?"

"No," I murmured.

"There's nothing more I can say, then. Just don't expect any help from me.'' With that he stood up, grabbed the unopened newspaper that was on the table, and strode into the living room.

At one time George had to be at school the same time I did, but for the past few years, ever since he had tenure, he was able to arrange his schedule so that his classes didn't begin until after nine. There were times I would have loved walking to school with him, but today I was glad we were on different schedules.

I ambled into the kitchen and lackadaisically fixed a bowl of Grape-Nuts with milk and sugar, stood over the kitchen counter, and forced myself to eat. I had managed to eat a few spoonfuls when Lucy burst into the kitchen dressed in her brown tweed suit and beige blouse—what she calls her ''make the deal'' suit.

''Morning, Sal,'' she greeted me. ''Wish me luck today. It could make all the difference.''

''Good luck,'' I mumbled, too deep in my own problems to worry about anyone else's.

''What I love is a good sendoff,'' Lucy laughed, popping some bread in the toaster.

I dumped my unfinished cereal in the garbage pail, stuck my bowl in the dishwasher without bothering to rinse it off, and went upstairs to get my things. On my way down Lucy brushed by me, complaining that she'd just snagged her stocking. ''Of all mornings,'' she griped.

It might seem on the surface that Lucy had totally recovered from our conversation, but I knew she was postponing judgment by not making any reference to it. I knew where George stood; he was inflexible. Lucy was my last hope, and I couldn't push her.

George was no longer in the living room when I came downstairs. He was probably in the kitchen, getting another cup of coffee, but there was so much tension be-

tween us that I didn't bother to look for him. For the first
time in as long as I could remember I made a point of *not*
saying good-bye.

I'm not sure how I got through the rest of the day,
because all I could think about was my appointment on
Friday. I'd saved a little money from my job last summer,
which I figured would pay for one visit. Of course, if I
didn't have anything to tell, I might as well cancel. Then
again, maybe Joey, who was assigned to my case, might
have some ideas on how I should proceed. Besides the
problems of logistics involved in my search, I was already
feeling the emotional cost that George had mentioned. But
I had psychologically turned a corner, and there was no
going back.

I'm not sure if it was coincidence or my imagination,
but George either avoided me or treated me like a polite
stranger. That afternoon we both arrived home before
Lucy. Normally we had a zillion things to talk about, but
we only exchanged hellos and then he buried his head in a
book and totally ignored me while I went into the kitchen
to fix a meatloaf that Lucy had planned for supper.

When Lucy came home a short time later, it was immediately obvious that she'd made the sale. "I did it, I did
it," she shouted. "The papers still have to be signed, but
Mrs. Taylor fell in love with the house, and they plan to
take occupancy next month."

"That's fabulous," my father said. "Let's break out a
bottle of champagne."

I emerged from the kitchen and forced myself to register
some enthusiasm. "Congratulations, Mother. I fixed the
meatloaf, and champagne will go great with it."

Lucy laughed at the ridiculous combination, but George
remained silent.

"As soon as I get out of this business suit, I can help

you in the kitchen, Sal." She, at least, was treating me the same as ever.

Then she turned to my father. "George, you're still in your jacket and tie. Why all the formality?"

"Forgot," he answered. "Been thinking about other things, I guess." He didn't look at me, but I knew that remark was intended for my ears.

"Well, let's both change. Sally shouldn't be stuck with preparing the whole meal."

"She can manage," George remarked coldly, following Lucy up the stairs.

I couldn't hear the exact words, but their muffled voices, which came from the bedroom, sounded angry. I didn't want to be caught eavesdropping, so I returned to the kitchen and began tossing the salad. A few minutes later, when Lucy came in, her mood had definitely changed. She had a tight, somber expression around her mouth that I long ago dubbed her "fight with Daddy" look. I knew I was responsible for whatever argument they had had, and it made me feel terrible. But there was nothing I could say.

Lucy took a bunch of carrots out of the fridge and stood over the sink meticulously scraping them, while I carefully proportioned the correct amounts of oil and vinegar for the salad dressing. We worked in silence, so intent on what we were doing that one would have thought we were on the brink of a great scientific discovery.

"We might as well talk," Lucy said. She had dumped the carrots in a bowl of cold water and pulled the kitchen stool close to where I was standing. She sat down wearily, her tenseness melting. One thing I could always count on with Lucy was that her bad moods never lasted.

"We have to," I agreed in a shaky voice.

"I just had a 'discussion' with your father," she said, half-smiling. "Daddy believes that nothing will be accomplished by your digging into your past, that you'll end up being hurt. I have to agree that there is that possibility.''

"I know, but that can't stop me."

"I know that nothing will stop you, and you're willing to take the risk of being hurt or disappointed or both."

"That's right. I just have to do this."

"I understand, Sally, and therefore I'm going to help you."

"You're going to help me?" I breathed excitedly.

"As much as I can. I want you to have peace of mind."

"You mean you'll give me names and addresses and all that?"

"I'll give you every piece of information I have, including a copy of your birth certificate."

"Oh, Mother, you're wonderful," I exclaimed. I felt as though a monstrous weight had been lifted from me. "But I wish Daddy would approve of what I'm doing."

"Be patient with him. I think he's afraid he'll lose you, and his way of handling that possibility is to be detached. When he finds out that your feelings for him haven't changed, he'll be fine."

"I hope you're right. I couldn't stand it if he turned on me."

"I don't think that will happen. Meanwhile, although he knows I'm going to help you, let's not keep talking about it in front of him."

"Right. Besides, we want to celebrate your sale." I was feeling up for the first time in ages, and I could honestly enjoy Lucy's success.

"This commission couldn't have come at a better time," Lucy remarked, getting up from the stool. "It will pay for the investigation."

"Oh, Mother," I sighed, "I feel awful about that."

"Look, Sal, it's my money, and that's the way I choose

to spend it," she asserted. "But now, let's finish cooking. The meatloaf will be overdone, and I haven't even put on the carrots."

All through supper Lucy described in detail the house she had sold—the number and size of the rooms, the four fireplaces, the dining room that could easily seat eighteen, the huge modern kitchen and pantry.

"It needs a family of ten to fill it, and there aren't so many of those around these days, especially ones that could afford this kind of house. I was just plain lucky."

Her enthusiasm was contagious and even George loosened up, joking about how when the Taylors are alone for dinner, there are only ten of them. He was civil but formal to me, which was better than suffering his silence or sarcasm.

After we'd finished eating, George announced that there was a TV program on sharks that he wanted to see, I mumbled something about doing my homework, and Lucy said she was exhausted and wanted to go to bed early. I trailed her up the stairs, and when she reached the top, she motioned to me to follow her into her bedroom. I could feel my heart beating faster, because I knew the moment of truth was coming.

She immediately headed for her closet and opened a small steel file cabinet that she kept on the floor, and withdrew an envelope yellow with age.

"This is a copy of your birth certificate and will provide you with all the vital statistics: place and date of birth, doctor's name, hospital. I think you should copy everything down and return it to me for safekeeping."

My hands were trembling as I took the envelope from her. "I'll do that right now." I tried to keep my voice calm. I wanted to be alone when I read that piece of paper that would change my life, and I think Lucy was sensitive to my need for privacy.

"Go ahead. I'm going to get ready for bed and then I'll come in and talk to you," she said.

I walked into my room as though I were holding a time bomb, turned on my desk lamp, sat down, opened the envelope, and carefully withdrew the small photocopy of my birth certificate that was enclosed. The very first line startled me: "Full name of child: Sally Delores Gordon." Naturally, I had never thought of myself as anyone but Sally Brighton, and I never knew I had a middle name. My birth date was accurate! June 10, 1968. Happily I didn't have to adjust to a different age! Then I saw that I had been born in Paterson, New Jersey, in General Hospital. That meant that the search would originate in the East and save traveling expenses. Then came more crucial information: My mother's name was Delores Gordon, age seventeen, and her address was 342 Willow Street, Paterson, New Jersey. Her first name, Delores, accounted for my middle name, and probably was the reason Lucy and George never told me about it. There was no information about my father, and I could only imagine that he had abandoned Delores and she refused to acknowledge his existence by not telling his name, age, or occupation. The certificate was signed by Emanuel Garfield, M.D.

I reread every word of that precious document more than twenty times so that I knew every scrap of information by heart. Then I typed it, word for word, and proofread it three times to make sure there were no errors. It was hard to believe that so few lines could have so much power over me. Delores, Delores, Delores, I kept repeating to myself, and tried unsuccessfully to picture her in my mind. If she was seventeen years older than me, she would be thirty-two, but that was all I had to go on.

I heard Lucy padding down the hall in her slippers, and as soon as she entered my room, I asked her if she'd ever met Delores.

"Never," she answered, tightening the belt of her old Chenille bathrobe. It was a faded pink robe, at least ten years old, and even though George had given her several new ones over the years to replace it, she couldn't bear to discard what she called her security blanket.

She took the spread off my bed and folded it neatly at the bottom, plumped the pillows into a backrest, and then stretched out.

"But you do know something about her," I said hopefully.

"I'm going to tell you the whole story, and then you'll know everything I know."

"Thank you," I said, an inadequate response to what must have been a painful memory for Lucy.

"When Daddy and I discovered after being married five years that we couldn't have a baby, we were desolate," she began. "We tried to convince ourselves that there were advantages to being childless—more money for trips and clothes and restaurants and theater, all those things that are supposed to make for a good life. But no matter how much we indulged ourselves, something was missing. This emptiness was constantly on my mind, but George didn't want to keep talking about it. You know what it's like to keep something bottled up?"

"Yep," I said, a little embarrassed that my mother was telling me all these personal things. But I didn't want her to stop.

"I had to talk about my feelings. You take after me that way," she added with a grin.

"That's right," I said seriously. "I'm just like you that way."

"Anyway, it was inevitable that I would tell my best and oldest friend, Beverly Newton, with whom I'd gone all through high school and college."

"I never heard you mention Beverly before," I remarked.

"That's because she married and moved out West, and we only write each other once a year, around Christmas."

"But she was your best friend?"

"Was, is, and always will be, because she's responsible for bringing you into our lives."

"How?" I couldn't wait for her to continue.

"Beverly was a nurse and worked in an internist's office in Paterson. One of the patients was a seventeen-year-old girl who had gotten pregnant and came to the office with her sister, who was nineteen. Apparently the parents were so upset at the disgrace their youngest daughter had brought to them that they left all the medical details to her older sister."

"You mean the pregnant girl wasn't married."

"That's right. She didn't have a husband, and her parents were ashamed of her. She must have been very gutsy to insist on having her baby without anyone's approval."

That seventeen-year-old pregnant unmarried girl was my biological mother, and I felt a rush of pride when I thought how much courage it took for her to give birth to me. But then why did she reject me?

"If she had been really gutsy, she never would have given me up," I said.

"That's not true," Lucy defended her. "I think it takes even more courage to admit that you can't take care of a child and, in spite of the heartbreaking wrench, give the baby to someone else."

"Maybe so, if you look at it that way," I conceded. "But go on."

"The day of Delores's first visit to Dr. Garfield, Beverly routinely took down her history, discovered that Delores had no husband and no means of supporting herself or a child, and that she planned to put her child up for adoption. Beverly thought of us immediately, for she knew how desperate we were to have a baby, and that night she called to tell us about Delores. We were so excited that that was all we could talk about, and we told Beverly to do everything she could to help us adopt the baby.''

"Wasn't there a lot of legal stuff to go through?"

"Everything was working in our favor, because Beverly's boyfriend, who she eventually married, was a lawyer, and he drew up an agreement that was satisfactory to all of us."

"Didn't you want to meet Delores before you made any decision about taking her baby?"

"I was tempted, but George was against the idea. He argued that it would be better all around if we didn't know each other. He was right, too, because from the very beginning we felt you were *our* baby and no one else's. I've never regretted that decision."

"Did you find out anything about Delores?"

"Beverly told us all we needed to know—that she was from a respectable family, was in perfect physical shape, and that she would undoubtedly have a healthy baby."

"And you got me when I was only two days old?"

"That's right. You were hand-delivered by Beverly, and I can honestly say it was the happiest day of my life."

Lucy stopped talking and there was a faraway look in her eyes. I knew she was reliving those early dramatic moments. I was quiet too, trying to sort out all my conflicting feelings. I could identify with Delores, who wasn't much older than I was right now when she gave birth to me; I could also see that I'd filled an enormous gap in Lucy and George's lives.

"I guess this is a lot to take in all at once, Sally, but I didn't want to hold back anything," Lucy said, reading my mind.

"I appreciate that. I'm just sorry that I have to put you through all this. It's not your fault."

"The circumstances of your birth aren't your fault either. And the more I think about it, the more I understand your need to know the truth."

She stood up, then came over to me, and without saying another word kissed me on the forehead and left the room.

I watched her leave, thinking that she couldn't have put it any better. I was searching for my identity, my roots, my genetic links, but what it all came down to was a need to know the truth.

Chapter 10.

I kept Nina and Eric informed about everything relating to my search, but I didn't want the entire world to know. Therefore I asked Nina to make up some excuse to Chris and Bambi about why I couldn't show up at Nick's the day of my appointment.

I didn't think classes would ever end Friday. When the last bell finally rang, I raced out of school to the railroad station, arrived five minutes early for the 3:10, fidgeted nervously on the platform until the train mercifully appeared. I settled into a seat next to a window and purposely put my canvas bag on the seat next to me so that no one would occupy it.

The train was a local, and the ride interminable, although it took less than thirty minutes to pull into Grand Central Station. I had plenty of time to reach my destination on West Forty-Fifth Street, but I couldn't help running all the way. Finders Inc. was located on the second floor, Room 24, of a seedy-looking building. There was an elevator, but it was in use and I was too impatient to wait for it, so I climbed the stairs, trying not to be disheartened by the peeling pale green walls and grimy banister. An arrow indicated Room 24, which was at the end of the dimly lit hall. Holding my breath in fear and suspense—I felt like I was a bad actor in a Grade B movie—I pressed the bell and grasped the doorknob.

There was a buzzing sound immediately. I opened the door and stumbled into the office. It took a few seconds for me to adjust to the room, which was startlingly bright after the dark corridor. The walls were bright yellow, adorned with colorful posters, and the furniture was Danish modern, surprisingly less tacky than I suspected after my first impression of the building.

"Hello, honey. You must be Sally Brighton." I couldn't mistake that nasal voice. It belonged to the person I'd spoken to over the phone. She was seated behind a desk with an elaborate phone system in front of her. A sign on her desk read ELIZABETH KANE.

"Hello," I said weakly.

"Everyone calls me Betty," she remarked. "I'll tell Joey you're here." She pressed one of the many buttons on the phone setup and announced my presence, while I sat down on a naugahyde chair and tried to hide my nervousness. I picked up a copy of *People* magazine, but all the pictures looked blurry to me, so I put it right down again.

"He's with a client now, but he'll be finished in about five minutes. Meanwhile, you can give me some vital statistics. I already have your name and age. Now I need your address and telephone number."

I told her, and then she asked, "How are you going to

pay for this?'' Betty looked tougher than she really was—too much mascara, and frizzy hair that had been over-peroxided.

''My mother's going to pay,'' I replied.

''That's nice, Sally, but how? Your first visit you must pay in cash; no checks or plastic cards. After that, we can make some other arrangement.''

''How much do you charge?'' I tried to sound business-like, but I couldn't keep a tremor out of my voice.

''The first visit will cost you fifty dollars.''

''Fifty dollars,'' I repeated, panicking because I had only brought twenty-five and I had visions of going home with nothing accomplished.

Betty sensed my dismay and suggested that maybe some allowance could be made this time, providing I paid half now and wrote an IOU for the rest.

''That would be terrific, because I have enough to pay half and I already have my return ticket home.''

''That's good. Now the cost of the investigation depends on how many hours are spent in the field and in the office.''

''In the field. What's that?''

Betty sighed wearily and explained that preliminary research took place in the office—making phone calls and writing letters—but that fieldwork meant knocking on doors and asking questions. ''It doesn't mean picking berries,'' she added facetiously, but there was a twinkle in her eye.

''In the field costs more than in the office, I guess.''

''You guessed it, kiddo. Like double.''

''And there's no way of knowing how long it will take.''

''Right again. It can take two weeks—I think that happened once that I've heard of—or twenty years. Most people give up after a couple of years, but some make it a lifetime occupation.''

"Do most the people who come here find the person they're looking for?"

"That depends."

I must have looked crestfallen—I guess I'd hoped she'd been more encouraging—because she quickly added, "We must be successful some of the time or we'd be out of business."

Just then a small, nice-looking, prematurely gray-haired woman came out of an inner office. She wore no makeup and she was pretty except for her bloodshot eyes. I realized she'd been crying. She stopped in front of Betty's desk, dug in her handbag for her wallet, and pulled out some bills.

"How's it going, Mrs. Gabriel," Betty asked, as she took the money.

"I'm almost ready to give up. For all I know, my husband has changed his name and moved to another part of the world. There's not a trace of him."

"Never know what can turn up."

"That's what I keep telling myself. But one month more of this investigation is all I can afford." She sighed and headed for the door.

"I'll see you next week," Betty said, and turned to pick up her phone, which was buzzing.

"Guess so," Mrs. Gabriel muttered and let herself out.

"You're next," Betty looked at me and pointed to a short hallway. "First door on your right."

My legs felt like jelly but they managed to propel me into Joey's office, which was small but cheery—the same yellow walls and more posters. And just seeing Joey put me at ease. He wasn't nearly as old and gruff as I had expected. He had curly dark hair, penetrating brown eyes, and a very pronounced dimple, which deepened when he smiled. He stood up from behind his desk as soon as I walked in and extended his hand to me. He was on the short side, but had a stocky compact frame and an air of authority that made me feel secure. After we shook hands—mine was clammy with fear—he told me to take a seat.

"Everybody who comes here is scared at first," he said, "but there's really nothing to be afraid of. We do our best and either we succeed or we don't. Right?"

"Right."

"The absolute worst thing that can happen is that we don't find the person our client is looking for. You must learn to live with whatever happens. If that lady who was just here doesn't find her husband, she'll have to give up on him and start a new life."

"Right," I said again, and wondered if I was capable of any other response.

"Anyhow, let's not think negatively. First of all, let me introduce myself. My name is Joseph Brinn, but everyone calls me Joey."

"And I'm Sally Brighton."

"Hi, Sally, and welcome to Finders Inc. I know you're looking for your mother—we'll call her your birth mother because that's the most accurate description."

I nodded my head.

"Now, I trust you've told your adoptive parents about your plan and they'll be cooperative?"

"My mother, yes. She's told me everything she knows and has even given me a copy of my birth certificate. My father," I added forlornly, "told me I was on my own and won't even talk about it."

"They're both acting out of love for you, in their own way."

"You think so?"

81

"I'm sure of it."

It was good to hear Joey, an outsider, say that, and I found myself relaxing for the first time in days. He encouraged me to talk about myself and my feelings, in addition to telling him everything I knew. I repeated the story Lucy had told me of how desperately she and George had wanted a baby, and how Beverly had made all the arrangements.

Joey took notes the whole time I was talking, and then double-checked to make sure he had written everything correctly. Then I showed him the copy of my birth certificate, and he studied it carefully.

"We've got a lot to work with, Sally—more than usual," he surmised. "But I don't want to be overly encouraging. For one thing, your birth mother may have moved to a different part of the country, or even to another part of the world. If she's married, she undoubtedly has a new name. Also, there's the possibility that she may not be alive."

I gasped when he said that, and he quickly added, "We've got to think positively, but you should be prepared. I'm going to cull through this information and figure out the best way to proceed. One thing that's missing is Beverly's address. If Lucy writes her every year, she must have it."

"I'll call you tonight, as soon as I get home, and give it to you."

Joey laughed. "We're closed at night. Call Monday after nine and leave it with Betty. Our hours are nine to five."

When he mentioned the time, I glanced at my watch and was amazed to see it was after five o'clock. "I can't believe a whole hour has gone by," I exclaimed. "When should I come back?"

"You've given me a number of names to work with: birth mother's, the doctor's, Beverly's. Until I check out these sources, there's no reason for you to set up another appointment."

"How will I know what's happening?"

"I'll call you on the phone. When is the best time?"

"I'm usually home at five, even if I stay after school for extracurricular stuff."

"That's when I'll call, then, as soon as I find out anything. But you must be patient. One of the toughest things for me to get across to people, young or old, is that this all takes time."

"I know. And even if you find her, she may not want to see me."

"That's brave of you to face that possibility, Sally. But remember, finding that out is also valuable."

"I know that too."

"Don't look so grim," Joey said, and smiled reassuringly. "You've taken an enormous step, and your decision to begin the search is half the battle." He stood up and held out his hand. This time I could return his warm handshake.

"Thanks for everything, Joey," I said, and turned toward the door.

"One more thing," he advised. "Let me worry about this now, and you go about your life."

Chapter II.

Going about my life and letting Joey worry was more easily said than done, but I did the best I could. George didn't ask me anything about my visit to Finders Inc.—he acted as though he didn't know about it—but as soon as we were alone, Lucy wanted to know everything. She gave me Beverly's current address, which I took to school with me on Monday and phoned in to Betty after my first class. I had set the wheels in motion, and there was nothing left for me to do but wait.

One benefit of my having talked to Joey was that I no longer felt like a weirdo because of my search, and I didn't have to be so secretive. The following Friday at Nick's, when we had our usual rap session, I told Chris and Bambi about it. Chris, in her matter-of-fact way, said it seemed like an obvious thing to do, and Bambi thought of all the dramatic aspects.

"Maybe you're the daughter of royalty and your father, who is an Italian count, would have had to forsake his fortune in order to claim you as his own."

"Not likely," I said, but I couldn't help smiling at the idea.

"Or maybe," she continued, "your mother is a famous movie actress, or author, or politician, or artist, or . . ."

Bambi looked deadly serious, but we were all laughing so hard, especially me, that she was forced to wind down. It was the first time in weeks that I was able to laugh at myself, and I realized how uptight I'd been. On the way home, Nina remarked happily that she'd noticed a difference in me and she was so glad I was able to talk about myself and what I was doing.

"It's really wonderful the way everyone's reacted. Except for George, everyone understands," I told her. "One of my problems has been that I believed, until I spoke to Joey, that I was the only kid in the world who was curious enough to do something *actively* about their adoption. He said he's handled a lot of cases like mine, and there are probably zillions of other adopted people who wonder all the time about their origins but never do anything about them."

"I guess we all think we're the only person in the world who's going through certain things," Nina mused. "Like the first time I ever held a boy's hand all through a movie. It was a Western, but that's all I remember. I was so conscious of Teddy Reynolds, the cutest boy in second grade, holding my hand that I had no idea what was happening on the screen."

"You never told me about Teddy. Whatever happened to him?"

"The following week he spent all his time hanging

around with Wendy, an adorable blond third-grader, and he acted as though he didn't know me."

"Maybe you didn't hold hands right."

"Probably not," she grinned, and then we both cracked up.

We'd come to the intersection where we had to separate, so we promised to call each other and went our own way. I smiled to myself the rest of the way home, thinking about Nina and her second-grade romance.

It felt so good not to be serious for a change and I was actually humming as I let myself into the house. The delicious smell of brownies wafted into the hall, and I knew Lucy was in the kitchen baking.

"Hi, sweetie," she called to me. "You're just in time to lick the bowl."

I went into the kitchen, kissed her on the cheek, and even before I took off my parka I went to work on scraping the sides of the bowl. As I licked the spoon I was thinking that since there was no longer any necessity to talk about the search, at least for the present, I could go about my life normally. Lucy wisely didn't dwell on the subject, and George pretended it hadn't happened. I told Eric the details of everything that had transpired, and we both agreed not to talk about it until I heard from Joey.

That night Eric was having some kids over to watch *The Great Santini* on Home Box Office. I went to his house after supper, and Bobby and his most recent girlfriend had already settled into the upstairs family room. Bobby, as always, greeted me like we hadn't seen each other for years, and then introduced me to Stacy Bidwell. I know its wrong to make snap judgments, but it was impossible not to have the impression that Stacy was a super snob. Her long, honey-colored hair that appeared to be ironed, high cheekbones, and tall narrow build gave her the look of a highly bred racehorse.

"Hi, Stacy," I greeted her.

She didn't bother to say hello, just plunged right in with, "I don't recall seeing you around. What grade are you in?"

"Tenth," I answered.

"That explains it. I don't happen to know any tenth-graders."

Bobby, who rarely seemed embarrassed in any situation, tried to cover up Stacy's arrogance by getting onto another topic. "Hey, Sal," he began, "I understand you're launched on a major quest."

"A what?" I asked innocently, not really wanting to hear the answer.

"You know, I hear you're looking for your blood mother."

I knew he was trying to be amusing, but the way he put it made me very uncomfortable. It was no secret anymore, and since Bobby was Eric's best friend, I couldn't expect them not to talk about me; I would have done the same. Still, bringing up the subject in front of Stacy, a complete stranger, made me very uneasy. I hoped by some miracle Stacy had tuned out, but instead she looked at me with new interest.

"You're adopted?" she inquired. "That must present all sorts of problems."

For the moment, I was speechless. Eric, wanting to rescue me, suddenly put on his "host" act and, totally ignoring Stacy's comment, asked if he could get anyone something to drink.

"I've got a wide assortment of sodas here," he said,

pointing to a tray filled with soft drinks, an ice bucket, and glasses.

"I'll take hemlock," Bobby groaned, and I knew that was his way of apologizing for being so insensitive.

But Stacy was indifferent to my reaction and used my predicament to sound off.

"I have an older cousin who's adopted—she's in her twenties—and she wanted to find her 'blood' mother, as Bobby put it. Her adoptive parents were furious and wouldn't help her, so she did the whole thing on her own."

"What happened?" I couldn't resist asking, no matter how painful.

"She had enough clues, and after a year she did get in touch with her mother, the one who gave her life."

"What then?"

"Her real mother didn't want anything to do with her—told her she was just a bad memory. And in the process she got her adoptive parents really upset. Their relationship has never been the same."

"That's just one case," Eric observed. He had seated himself on the couch next to me and taken my hand in his.

"And it's probably not typical." Bobby was no longer interested in protecting his date.

"Besides, I've made up my mind," I asserted, reinforced by Eric's and Bobby's comments.

"I'm just trying to be helpful," Stacy explained haughtily. "I thought you might like to reconsider pursuing this, once you heard my cousin's experience."

To my amazement, as well as everyone else's, I found myself saying, "I appreciate your telling me this, Stacy, and I'm sure what happened to your cousin isn't all that unusual. But if the same thing happens to me, I'm ready. What you don't understand is that knowing the truth, even if it's painful, is more important than not knowing. And if I find out nothing, at least I will have tried. It's known as risk-taking.''

"I hope you know what you're doing, that's all," she countered, but I knew I'd won a moral victory, especially when Eric squeezed my hand and smiled his approval.

"Who needs HBO when we've got our own drama right here," Bobby said, laughing.

"I almost forgot. You did come here for the movie," Eric said, glancing at his watch. "And it's about to start." He stood up, flicked off the lights, and switched on the set.

When he sat down next to me again and put his arm around my shoulder, I felt a new kind of strength. Just a few months ago I would have cowered before Stacy's hostility, but her dire warnings didn't faze me. If anything, I felt I'd been tested and the results proved I could cope.

The fact that I had handled Stacy's attack made the waiting game easier. Whenever I had doubts about whether I was doing the right thing, I recalled in minute detail the Stacy scene, and it always made me feel better. There were still moments when I had anxiety attacks or was stricken with guilt. And I wasn't always so sure that I wouldn't be shattered—temporarily, anyway—if I never found Delores or, worse, if I did find her but she didn't want to see me.

I went for days trying my best not to wonder about what progress Joey was making. I resisted calling him, although occasionally I had the ridiculous notion that maybe he had forgotten me. Then, one Saturday, three weeks after I first saw him, I received a letter that allayed my fears. We were having breakfast, and there were three staccatto raps on our door knocker, which was the mailman's signal. George went to pick up the mail and, when he returned, shoved a thin white envelope towards me.

"For you," he remarked tonelessly. "Junk mail."

"Thanks, Daddy," I said, curious as to why he seemed annoyed.

Then I noticed the return address, Finders Inc., and I realized that George, too, had been trying hard to live with a disturbing situation. He'd been reasonably successful, but this reminder was a fresh jolt for which he wasn't prepared. He picked up his coffee mug and abruptly left the room.

"What's that all about?" Lucy asked me in a low voice.

I had opened the envelope and was trying to absorb the itemized bill. The total amount for three weeks' work came to two hundred and seventy-five dollars.

"Two seventy-five," I muttered, and my face must have registered the shock. The assurance that Joey had remembered me was a great relief, but the cost threw me.

"What's wrong?" Lucy asked. "You've turned white."

"This," I said, sliding the bill toward her.

She read it quickly and her reaction was instantaneous. "What did you expect? Five hours' work, plus twenty-five owed on your first visit. I think that's fair."

"You do?" I couldn't believe how casual she was.

"We'll pay till the money runs out." She shoved the bill in the pocket of her bathrobe.

"But Mother, it's costing so much." I was really bothered.

"Let me take care of it, will you?"

I nodded my head, knowing there was no alternative.

Then she added briskly, "Let's clear away these dishes.

I have to do some paperwork in the office this morning and I'd like to get there before ten.''

"I'll clean up," I volunteered. That's the least I could do, I thought. I needed to do something to alleviate my guilt feelings.

"I'll let you," Lucy agreed, smiling, as though she could read my mind.

Chapter 12.

On the surface, we went back to behaving like a typical family. I counted on there being no more "scenes" as long as we avoided the mention of Finders, Inc. in front of my father. I never talked about the investigation with my friends, who knew exactly what was going on and realized there wasn't anything else for me to tell them. That didn't mean for a minute that I didn't think about it, and fantasize about the phone call from Joey. Another few weeks passed, and I was beginning to think it would never happen.

On a Thursday, the last week in February, I was in the kitchen preparing lasagne. It was going to be a late day for Lucy, and George had a faculty meeting, so I had volunteered to fix dinner from scratch. I had just finished arranging the layers of noodles, mozzarella, chopped meat, and tomatoes in the pyrex baking dish, when the phone rang. Nina, knowing I had the kitchen detail, had promised to call not only to distract me from my domestic duties, but to fill me in on her burgeoning romance. This was the first time Nina had ever wanted to get involved, and even I was surprised that she'd gone ape, so suddenly, over a guy.

His name was Dennis Klein. She'd met him in an advanced class in computer science, which was mostly for upperclassmen. Since the class was small, it was easy to talk to everyone, and Nina soon discovered that Dennis was exactly her type. He was quick-witted, scientifically brilliant, and indifferent to women, but she was prepared to change the latter characteristic. She claimed he had the kind of looks most girls wouldn't find attractive but she flipped over. He looked like an intellectual: high forehead, prominent nose, intense brown eyes. Nina told me that they never talked about anything but computer programming, but in their last class he had suggested that they "program" each other to meet outside of school. Nina inferred that this was his way of asking her out, so she readily agreed. But nothing happened after that. She was hopeful that since he was such a whiz at numbers he might figure out how to find hers, and perhaps dial it.

"If that doesn't happen," she pleaded on the way home from school, "you've got to help me dream up a way to galvanize him."

"I'll try," I promised, and the whole time I was in the kitchen cooking, I thought about Nina's problem. I even came up with a solution, which I couldn't wait to present. Therefore, when the phone rang I was so sure it was Nina that instead of saying hello, I said, "I've got it."

"Got it?" a nasal voice echoed.

"What?" I asked stupidly, completely discombobulated when I realized it wasn't Nina.

"Is this Sally Brighton?" The twang was unmistakable, and I was completely unnerved.

"Betty," I gasped. "It's you!"

"It's me all right, kiddo. For a minute I thought I had the funny farm."

"I'm sorry," I sputtered. "I didn't think you'd ever call. I mean, I knew you would, but it seemed like years and I—"

"Not quite years," she interrupted, "but let me connect you to Joey."

"Joey," I muttered, trying to remember to breathe. This was the call I'd been praying for and dreading at the same time. Although I'd never passed out in my life, I had a fleeting notion that if I didn't compose myself, I might faint. I pulled the kitchen stool toward me and sat down, figuring I'd be less likely to conk out if I got off my feet.

"Hello, Sally, how are you?" Joey asked warmly, as though he didn't hold my fate in his hands.

"Fine," I replied. "What's happened?" I couldn't take time to be polite.

"Well, we've taken a number of steps, and I wanted you to know where we're at."

"Yes, please tell me." I was clutching the receiver to my ear with both hands in order to stop my shaking.

"First we contacted Beverly, and she was—"

"Did she tell you where Delores is?" I interrupted.

"Slow down, Sal, I want you to know the procedure."

"Sorry," I apologized. "I'm just so excited."

"I know. Now, as I was saying, we got in touch with Beverly, and she was very cooperative. She fully believes that what you're doing is correct."

"That's a relief," I said, and forced myself to relax my hold on the phone so that my knuckles were no longer white.

"You're right. If she had put obstacles in our way, everything would take a lot longer."

"What did she tell you?"

"She wrote me a long, detailed letter—" he began, but just then I heard the front door open.

"Anybody home?" It was my father, and I knew I had to get off the phone.

"Can't talk now," I told Joey quickly, keeping my voice as low as possible. "My father just came home."

"I understand. When can you call me?"

"Can't," I murmured, trying not to get too agitated.

"Then when can you come in?"

"Today is Thursday. How about tomorrow at four?" I thought I'd die if I had to wait until next week.

There was a pause that seemed endless, but finally he said, "I know how anxious you are, so I'll rearrange my schedule and see you then."

"Wonderful!" I exclaimed. "But tell me, have you found her?" I couldn't sleep all night if I didn't know the answer.

"Not yet, Sally, but we're on the track."

"That's something," I sighed.

"See you tomorrow."

"Bye, Joey, and thanks." I hung up the receiver, but stayed glued to the stool. George, fortunately, had gone directly upstairs, probably to change his clothes, which gave me a few minutes to recover. *We're on the track, we're on the track* was a refrain that kept going through my head. I couldn't help but be optimistic, although I knew that was premature. There were so many possible snags.

Then I heard Lucy opening the front door, and greeting George, who must have been coming down the stairs. I leapt off the stool and proceeded to slice the Italian bread, a good idea before putting it in the oven, according to Lucy. When they both came into the kitchen, I was hard at work, trying not to show the emotional effect of Joey's call.

"Looks like you're doing a great job," Lucy remarked.

"I didn't know you were home," George said. "Didn't you hear me come in?"

"I was on the phone," I answered. It wasn't a lie, but I couldn't look him in the eye.

"When do we eat?" he asked. I was relieved that he didn't quiz me further about why I didn't say hello as soon as he came home.

"About forty minutes. That's how long it takes for the lasagne."

"Time for you to have a beer," Lucy said.

"At least one," George chuckled.

It was the kind of remark that he used to make with me all the time, and I felt a pang of remorse. Would George ever kid with me again, or would we spend the rest of our lives in this semiformal relationship?

George took a beer from the fridge and disappeared into the living room, saying he wanted to see the six o'clock news.

"Go ahead, dear. I'll be right in."

Lucy never pressed me into telling her things, but she always allowed opportunities for me to talk. The truth was, I couldn't wait to tell her about Joey's call, and I repeated my conversation with him almost word for word.

"I'm going to see him tomorrow after school, and then I'll know more," I finished.

"Good, Sal. I'm glad things are beginning to happen. Thanks to Beverly, there are probably plenty of clues."

"Thanks to you for having such a great friend, and for helping me. I just don't know what I'd do—"

"Enough!" Lucy interrupted. "Let's just hope everything works out. Right now, I want to get out of these clothes and join Daddy with a beer.''

As I watched her leave the kitchen and then went back to my bread slicing, I thought about Stacy's cousin and how alone she must have felt. I'm not sure how I would cope if both my adoptive parents disapproved. Now that I had a better perspective on what was happening, I saw the irony in the situation: Lucy, who had the most to lose, was offering me the most support. I really didn't know what I'd do without her.

Chapter 13.

Betty was wise-cracking and friendly as ever when I arrived ten minutes early at Finders Inc. on Friday. I felt totally unhinged, but she must have been used to distraught clients because she pretended not to notice.

"You must be Joey's pet," she said. "He never changes appointments, but because of you he rearranged his life— ate lunch at his desk, had me juggling clients around like crazy, and I even had to cancel someone."

"Oh, no," I groaned. "I hope it wasn't Mrs. Gabriel." For some reason I felt a strange kinship with her and believed my destiny was locked in with hers, probably because she was the first person I'd ever met who was also looking for someone.

"We're finished with Mrs. G. Case closed more than two weeks ago."

"What happened?" I asked anxiously.

"Well, I'm really not supposed to talk about anybody's case, but I don't think it could hurt for you to know that her husband showed up on her doorstep one day. Nothing to do with Finders Inc. Just decided he wanted to return home."

"That's terrific," I exclaimed, thinking for sure that was a good omen for me. "Can you tell me why?"

"Something about his having a mid-life crisis but realizing how much she meant to him and—"

The intercom phone buzzed, cutting our conversation short.

"Joey's ready for you."

"Thanks," I said, and hurried into his office.

"Good to see you, Sal," he greeted me. "Sit down and we'll get right to work."

I slid into the chair next to his desk and eagerly awaited his report. A large manila folder was lying open in front of him and he had apparently been jotting down notes on a legal-size pad.

"I want to know everything," I urged, peering at his notes but unable to decipher them upside down.

"And I'm going to tell everything," he answered, smiling at my impatience. "I wrote Beverly immediately, but she was on vacation for a couple of weeks so we didn't get a reply until ten days ago."

"But she doesn't know where Delores is, you said."

"No, she lost track of her soon after you were born because that's when Beverly married and moved to California."

"What about Dr. Garfield? Maybe he knows something."

"I thought of that, too," he said trying to keep a serious face, and making me feel like an idiot for suggesting such an obvious possibility.

"Did you reach him?"

"I asked Beverly for his address—his hospital and his home—but unfortunately he is deceased. He died two years ago."

"That's terrible," I cried. I wasn't upset about his dying, because he didn't mean anything to me, but I knew he might have been a link to Delores.

"The good news I learned is that his wife is still alive, and resides at the address Beverly has given me."

"Does she know anything?"

"I wrote her, and yesterday morning I received an almost illegible scrawl in the mail. The gist of it was that she hates to put anything in writing—she's probably a bit senile—but that she's willing to talk to me in person. She hates the phone, but she likes visitors and 'receives' every day since her husband passed away."

"And you're going to see her?"

"I'm going tomorrow, which is Saturday, and although it's not usually a work day for me, I have too many office appointments next week to take off."

"Oh, Joey," I shouted, "that's fantastic. Maybe Mrs. Garfield will know where Delores is."

"One of the reasons I wanted to see you, although I know it's not easy for you to get here, was to keep you informed. But also, I want to impress on you that there's still a long way to go. I'm quite sure Mrs. Garfield doesn't have all her marbles, and she may misremember things that happened fifteen years ago. And she may know nothing about Delores. After all, she was just one of many patients of Dr. Garfield's."

"If she doesn't remember anything, then what?" I asked sullenly.

"We'll think of another track. I'm reluctant to seek out Delores's parents because they disowned her and would only be hostile to this kind of investigation."

"Who else is there to ask?"

"There's Delores's sister, but we're up against the same obstacles."

"We'll never find her," I whimpered.

"Sally," Joey said firmly, "a minute ago you were too hopeful, but there's no reason to despair. There are still things we can do, including knocking on doors of neighbors where Delores once lived. You'd be amazed how one scrap of information from someone who knew the family can put us on the right track."

I nodded my head, trying to believe him.

"Anyhow," he continued, "our best bet for now is Mrs. Garfield. You can call me tomorrow night at my home and I'll tell you what happened."

"I can't wait," I said. Then I suddenly had a brainstorm. "Can I go with you?"

"To see Mrs. Garfield?" Joey was amazed at my suggestion.

"Yes. Maybe it would help if she saw how much I want to find Delores."

"Maybe you're right," Joey said thoughtfully. "It's not usual, and you'd have to get permission. Lucy would have to call me and say it's okay."

"I know she will."

"We have to drive to Paterson, you know. I've already told Mrs. Garfield I'd be there around eleven in the morning, before her other visitors arrive. No point in letting her think I don't believe she has a lot of people coming to see her."

"I'll come into Manhattan and meet you wherever you say." I could barely contain my excitement.

"No problem. I'll pick you up and then we'll shoot across the George Washington Bridge. Paterson is only about twenty minutes away, but we have to allow time to find her house."

"That's great!" I gleefully clapped my hands like a three-year-old, but then I froze.

"What's wrong?" Joey asked. "You look paralyzed."

"I just thought of something. George will freak out if you pick me up in front of our house. He knows what's happening, but he doesn't like to be reminded."

"Then why don't I pick you up somewhere else?" Joey suggested calmly.

"I never thought of that! Can you meet me at the shopping mall on 259th Street, in front of the drugstore?"

"I'll be there in my brown Datsun, ten o'clock sharp."

"Ten o'clock sharp," I echoed.

We said good-bye and I tried not to dance out of his office. Finally, I was totally involved. I was *doing* something, but in order to keep cool I kept reminding myself that, as Joey said, there was still a long way to go.

I was a bundle of nerves as we tooled along the George Washington Bridge, even though everything had gone without a hitch. Lucy, predictably, approved of my going with Joey and called him at home to let him know. Since I often leave the house early on Saturday, there was no problem about me getting away. Besides, George was less inclined than ever to ask me questions. Joey was right on time, and immediately assured me that he had a general idea where Mrs. Garfield lived.

"I've done all my homework," he boasted, handing me a detailed map of Paterson. He had indicated with a red Magic Marker our destination, and written an address at the edge of the map.

"We're heading for 3601 Banbury Street, right?"

"Right. You can tell me what to do after I hit Main Street. That's when the going gets tricky."

"I'll try." I was pleased that I could be useful and carefully studied the map, but as a navigator I was a dismal failure.

We found Main Street without any problem, but then there were a number of small side streets, too insignificant to put on the map, and we couldn't find Banbury. After driving around in a maze for at least ten minutes while I was reduced to silently biting my thumbnail, Joey conceded defeat and stopped at a gas station to ask for directions.

"End of the block," an unshaven crusty attendant said, shaking his head. He pointed straight ahead and looked at us as though we were escaped lunatics.

"Oh, really? Thanks, buddy." Joey smiled at him benignly and took off, while I had a fit of the giggles. Somewhere I had read that laughing is a cure for most maladies, and I was beginning to think it was true. It was only a few minutes later that we pulled up to 3601 Banbury, but I was feeling a lot more relaxed.

Mrs. Garfield's house, a small white Colonial, was in the center of the block. There were still traces of snow on the ground, but the path leading to the door had been well shoveled. Joey pressed the buzzer and I could hear the chimes of the bell ringing. We waited at least three minutes while I stamped my feet, trying to keep warm, and also to channel my impatience. Joey buzzed again, and I was losing heart when the door opened with the inside chain attached so that we couldn't possibly enter. A pair of bespectacled gray eyes, level with mine, peered at us, and a voice creaked, "What is it?"

"It's me, Joey, from Finders Inc., Mrs. Garfield. I told you I'd be coming today."

"Well, why didn't you say so?" she grumbled. "I've been waiting for you all morning. Put the tea kettle on and off six times already. People never on time these days." She unlatched the chain, and waved us in.

"Had a little trouble finding your house," Joey explained tactfully, although it was exactly eleven o'clock and we weren't a minute late.

"Glad of that," she cackled. "Not so easy to get robbed if they can't find my house."

As Mrs. Garfield reached in the vestibule closet for a couple of hangers, Joey winked at me and smiled. It didn't take long to see that we'd run into a certified character.

"I'll hang up our things," I offered, as she backed out of the closet.

"In my house, I do the hanging," she intoned, and promptly grabbed my parka. "Who're you anyway? That Finder's Inc. fellow, Joey he calls himself, didn't say anything about bringing a girl along. You his daughter or his secretary?"

"Neither," I replied. "I'm the girl who's looking for her mother, her birth mother, that is, Delores Gordon. My name is Sally Brighton."

She looked at me hard, as though she was making up her mind about me, but all she said was, "Amazing, amazing." When she finished putting our jackets in the closet, she ordered us to wait for her in the living room while she brought out the tea tray.

The living room was all lavender and old lace, with antimacassars covering the arms and backs of every chair and the couch. There was a dark oriental rug on the floor, and the mahogany furniture had been waxed to a high gloss. We hardly had time to sit down and take in our surroundings before Mrs. Garfield trotted in with a tea cart loaded with an assortment of homemade cookies and cakes.

"Now, Sally, you poor little thing, come over here and help yourself to a plate of goodies. You too, Joey, although you don't look like you need it."

It was hard not to laugh, she was so deadly serious, but we managed to contain ourselves and did exactly what she instructed. Once we'd settled down, balancing our teacups and dessert plates, Mrs. Garfield pulled a cigarette out of the flowered shift she was wearing and lit up. She looked like a frazzled Grandma Moses, and I wished I'd brought my camera.

Her eyes were bright and knowing, and I suspected that her battiness was more manufactured than real. I especially thought so when Joey broke the ice, saying, "You have a lovely home, Mrs. Garfield."

She retorted, "You didn't come here to socialize, Joey. Let's get down to cases." She leaned back in her overstuffed chair, inhaled deeply on her cigarette, and slowly blew rings into the air.

For the first time since I'd known him, Joey seemed taken aback, but he sensed that Mrs. Garfield didn't want to play games. "Can you tell us anything about Delores Gordon?" he began. "Sally decided about two months ago that she wanted to—"

Before he could finish his sentence, Mrs. Garfield interrupted. "Plenty."

"You know plenty about Delores?" My heart skipped a beat.

"My husband, bless his soul, told me everything about his patients. Not that I ever met them, but there wasn't a one that I didn't know well. I could tell you about everyone's ailment and the progress they were making. Sometimes I even advised Manny—Emanuel, that's my dear departed's name—what he should prescribe. One woman, I can't remember her name—very bad on names—was coming down with a different ailment every week. Found out her last child, her baby, had gone off to college and she had nothing to do. I told Manny to tell her to get off her seat and get a job. He did, she did, and she was cured. Lost a steady patient—prompt payer, too—but made someone happy. Think maybe I should have been a psychiatrist. Manny thought so too. Now where were we?"

"About Delores Gordon," Joey reminded her.

"Oh, yes. Very pretty kid, Manny told me, but disgraced her family. Oops, shouldn't say that to you, Sally, because you're a doll, I can see that. I'm sure Delores didn't think of you as a disgrace, either. Gave you away because she couldn't take care of you proper. Hope you like who she gave you to."

"I do, I do," I assured her. "Just need to find Delores if I can."

"Well, might as well get to the point. I tend to lose track sometimes. That's why I'm not allowed to drive. But my niece comes by every day to see if I need anything. I wasn't blessed with children, but my niece, Beezy, is wonderful to me."

"What about Delores Gordon?" Joey wanted to stop her from rambling.

"Oh, yes. Delores. She had this baby girl—you, it turns out, Sally—and then gave you away."

"Right, but what happened to Delores?" I held my breath.

"You wouldn't believe what happened. It was like a fairy tale. One of the best stories Manny ever told—except he never lived to see the ending. I might, though, now that you've sought me out."

"Please, Mrs. Garfield," I implored, "tell me where my mother is." I guess I sounded as desperate as I was feeling and finally got to her.

"She married Hamilton Brant."

"Hamilton Brant," Joey repeated, and jotted the name down on a pad he'd pulled out of his pocket.

"You've heard of him, I hope," Mrs. Garfield rattled on. "A millionaire, several times over. Known as the Copper King. That Delores did all right, considering the trouble she caused her parents. Oops, Sally, I didn't mean that. You don't look like trouble to me, just a sweet kid. Pretty, too."

"Thank you," I murmured. I had trouble holding back tears of relief and joy.

"Do you know where they live?" Joey was all business.

"Who?" Mrs. Garfield inquired.

"Mr. and Mrs. Hamilton Brant."

"Oh yes, that's who we were talking about. They probably have homes all over the world. He could afford it. Peru, St. Moritz, Paris, Rome—who knows?"

"But do they have a home here, in the States?" I thought she might have been imagining the international possibilities.

"Yes, I think so. Somewhere in New Jersey."

"New Jersey?" I screamed with glee.

"Not Paterson, my dear. Some fancy part—horse country. Scotch something, I think it is."

"Scotch Plains?" Joey asked eagerly.

"That's it! Scotch Plains! Plenty of big estates there. Wouldn't be surprised if they bred their own horses. With that kind of money—"

"Oh, Mrs. Garfield, you're wonderful," I exclaimed, and impulsively ran over to her and hugged her.

"There, there, pet, just trying to be helpful." She held

on to my arm with one hand, and with her other took a last drag on her cigarette before grinding it out in the ashtray. Then she stood up and hugged me back hard. I realized this deceptively frail little woman was strong as iron.

But then she turned quickly away, busying herself with the tea dishes, and I was sure she brushed away a tear with the back of her hand.

Chapter 14.

As soon as we climbed into the car, I bubbled with delight over our good luck. Joey was equally overjoyed with the results, but he had to behave professionally. "There might still be obstacles that will prevent a reunion," he cautioned me.

"I know, Joey, but at least I know where to reach Delores."

"Can't deny that—providing Mrs. Garfield's information is correct."

"It has to be!" I insisted. "I can call her as soon as I get home. Get her number through Information."

"You could, but I don't advise it. Hearing from you will be a real shocker, and the best way to introduce yourself is through the mail."

"I guess you're right. I have to find her address, then."

"I already thought of that. I noticed a post office on

Main Street, and we'll stop there now and check out a Scotch Plains directory.''

"Oh, Joey, I never would have thought of that!'' I could have kissed him.

Two minutes later, he double-parked in front of the local post office and stayed behind the wheel while I leapt out of the car and raced into the building. The New Jersey telephone books were piled on a center table, and it was easy to find the suburban directory containing the Scotch Plains section. I frantically turned to the B's as though my life depended on it. Joey had planted a kernel of doubt in my mind about the accuracy of Mrs. Garfield's statements, and it was growing. I had trouble focusing my eyes on the small print, mainly because my adrenalin was racing. But there, in the third column, was the name H. Brant, and the address; Walnut Farms.

"It's here, it's here," I shouted, unable to contain my outburst, and not even caring that several people smiled at me indulgently.

I hurried back to the car, muttering aloud, "I found it, I found it.''

"Excellent," Joey beamed. "The technical part of this mission has been accomplished in short order.''

"Thanks to you.''

"And thanks to you, too. You've been a first-rate client, and your going with me today was inspired. I'm not so sure Mrs. Garfield would have been so agreeable if you hadn't been there.''

"I'm not so sure either," I admitted. "But now you've got to help me write the letter.''

"You don't need me for that," Joey protested.

"But what'll I say?" I was so afraid of blowing it, after having gone this far.

"Just say what's on your mind, in your own words.''

"But what if I say the wrong things and scare her off?"

"Sally, you've said all the right things so far if today is an example of your diplomatic talents. I'd be doing you a disservice if I interfered."

"I s'pose," I replied, my ego bolstered by his confidence in me, but still worried. Then I wondered whether I should ask Nina or Eric to help me compose the perfect letter.

In answer to my thoughts, Joey remarked, "What goes on now is between you and your birth mother. You have to speak for yourself. No one else can do it."

I thought that over and knew he was right. What happened now was between me and Delores.

When I got home, it was almost three o'clock and the house was empty. Lucy had left a note on the kitchen counter saying she and George wouldn't be home until six. I was happy to be alone, with three hours of complete privacy in which to write Delores.

I pulled out the pale blue stationery printed in navy blue with my name and address across the top. My Aunt Judy had given me a hundred sheets and envelopes for Christmas, and at the time I thought it would take me a lifetime to use it up. It was much too formal for my friends, but I thought it was perfect for writing lost mothers.

I settled down at my desk and carefully addressed the envelope. Then I sat with my pen poised in the air, the blank stationery in front of me, and realized I was already completely stymied as to how to begin. I was sure no book of etiquette, even if I had one, could inform me of the proper greeting. Delores, who had given me life, was a complete stranger. Should I call her Mrs. Brant? That seemed much too formal, even though I didn't know her. I might start out with "Dear Mother," but that seemed bizarre and might turn her off forever if she didn't want to acknowledge that she was my mother. I decided calling her Delores was the least offensive designation. I knew some parents didn't find kids calling them by their first names acceptable, but this situation was unique.

"Dear Delores," I began. Then miraculously everything poured out easily and I didn't even have to recopy my original version.

> My name is Sally Brighton, and I am your daughter, originally named Sally Delores Gordon. I've been wondering for a long time about you, my biological mother, and finally decided to do something about finding you. I started my search almost two months ago, and have traced you through Dr. Garfield's widow, who knew where you were living.
>
> I have been warned that sometimes mothers who have given up their baby for adoption never want to see that child again, or be reminded of his or her existence. I hope with all my heart that you will want to see me.
>
> Please write me, as soon as you can, and tell me your decision. I'll meet you wherever you say.
>
> Yours,
> Sally

I folded the letter and placed it in the envelope. As I closed the self-sealing flap, I thought I was literally sealing my fate. I went into my parents' room and found a stamp in Lucy's desk. Next, I grabbed my doorkey and rushed out of the house without bothering to put on my parka. I ran all the way to the mailbox, which was at the end of our block, so intent on what I was doing that I didn't feel the cold. I slid the envelope into the slot, had the presence of mind to read the pick-up schedule—my letter would be collected at five o'clock—and hurried home. I had forgotten all about having lunch, but decided to fix some cocoa.

As I stirred the chocolate powder and milk, I was still high with what had been accomplished. "The search is over, the search is over," I kept repeating, not quite able to believe it. There was nothing more I could do, absolutely nothing. I recalled the line, "All things come round to him who will but wait." Please, I thought absurdly, please, Mr. Longfellow, be right!

I sat down on the kitchen stool and sipped my cocoa, reviewing in my mind all that had transpired in a relatively short time. I couldn't wait to tell Eric and Nina the news. That night Eric and I were going with a bunch of kids to a rock concert in White Plains and he was picking me up at seven. It was only five o'clock, so there was plenty of time for me to call him before George came. Then I would call Nina. I picked up the receiver and started to dial Eric's number, but something stopped me and I hung up before the connection was made. It may sound crazy, but I wanted my parents to be the first to know. George as well as Lucy. Slipping away from the house unobtrusively and making sneaky phone calls was getting to me. I didn't want to go on this way, no matter how tough it was. Before I had a chance to hedge on my decision, the back door opened and George came in.

"Hi, Sally," he said. "I dropped Mother off at the Manfelds. She's helping fix a surprise birthday dinner for Irene's sister and she won't be home for another hour."

He started to walk through the kitchen, taking his coat off, when I stopped him. "Hey, Daddy," I gulped. "I want to talk to you."

"What about?" he asked, standing in the threshhold of the door.

"I know you don't like to talk about it, and I hate to

113

upset you, but it's even worse if I don't tell you what's going on."

"The search, I suppose." He sounded resigned.

"Yes. I found out today where Delores lives, and I wrote her a letter saying I wanted to meet her."

"You've made quite a bit of progress."

"Yes," I exclaimed, unable to hide my enthusiasm.

"Look, Sally, you know I don't like any of this, but I have to admit one thing: you've got guts."

"You think so?" It was the first time in ages that George had said anything friendly to me, and I impulsively got up from the kitchen stool and was going to throw my arms around him to show my appreciation. But before I reached him, I could feel him stiffen and turn away from me.

I was momentarily crushed, but told myself I was expecting too much of him. Since he disapproved, there was no reason for him to be overjoyed at my success. But he did tell me I had guts, and in spite of his resistance, I knew that meant he was proud of me.

Everyone else was genuinely happy for me. Lucy couldn't believe the speed with which Joey and I operated; Nina remarked that I was so good at tracing people I should become a spy or an investigative reporter; and Eric, who had held my hand through the whole ordeal, helped me figure to the last hour when Delores would receive my letter and how soon I should expect a reply.

We decided that Tuesday morning was a reasonable time for my letter to reach her. If she replied immediately, I might hear from her by Thursday. That would be the optimum, but there were all sorts of contingencies that might delay her response. She might be out of town, she might take days to ponder over what she wants to say, and worst of all, she might not respond at all.

Again, there was a tacit agreement between me and my friends—I'd told Chris and Bambi all that had happened—that we wouldn't talk about my case. As soon as I heard from Delores, assuming I ever did hear, I would tell them.

I never especially thought about the mailman's schedule, but now it seemed incredibly cruel that he delivered our mail less than one hour after I had to leave for school. I was tempted to rush home Thursday during lunch period, but Nina talked me out of that. We were heading for the cafeteria together, and she reminded me that she hadn't kept me up-to-date on her romance with Dennis.

"How's it going?" I asked, and realized how self-involved I'd been.

"It's not going," she answered. "He still hasn't asked me out."

Then I remembered that I'd never gotten around to tell her my plan. So much had happened to me that I hadn't had time to think about anyone else's problem. "I had this great idea for you," I explained, "but then Betty, from Finders Inc., called, and I didn't get around to telling you, and I'm glad you reminded me because—"

"Never mind that. Tell me your idea."

"Since you're both into computers, I thought you could suggest that you go to the IBM exhibit together. George told me it's fascinating. It's in Manhattan, it'll get Dennis out of the classroom, and probably mean you'll have lunch somewhere."

"That's a genius idea!"

We had arrived at the cafeteria and took our place at the end of a long line. "Now that I've solved your problem, are you sure I shouldn't go home and pick up the mail? Maybe there's—"

"No way," she laughed. "You've simply got to be a nonthinker for the next few days. As my grandmother says,

115

'A watched pot never boils.' And besides, my problem isn't exactly solved. What if Dennis has already seen the IBM exhibit?''

"If he's as smart as you say he is, he'll go again."

"But what if he doesn't?" she persisted.

Her problem seemed so simple compared to mine. "I'll think up something else," I promised. "But what do I do if I don't hear from Delores?"

"There's nothing you can do," she admitted, "but there's no point in worrying. Now back to my problem with Dennis."

I realized then that Nina was doing her best to distract me, but that was only temporary. I couldn't stop being obsessed with the mail. Thursday, Friday, Saturday—and there were no signs. When I got home from school on Monday and found nothing on my desk—which is where Lucy always left any letters addressed to me—I was ready to cry. According to Eric's calculation, four days had passed during which I might have heard. I tried to psyche myself up for total disappointment, but somewhere I knew I would go through life wondering. Three more days passed, and what had begun as joyful anticipation had turned to a dull ache.

I no longer rushed home from school, and on Friday I went to Nick's as usual. My friends had never bugged me with questions, but I only thought it was fair to mention that I hadn't heard from Delores and considered the whole process an exercise in futility. They reminded me that making the attempt was very important. Still, I was back at square one, and there was no place to go. I had to accept the inevitable.

Lucy was already home when I let myself into the house, and she rushed out of the kitchen even before I had a chance to close the door. She looked unusually flustered, and for an instant I was sure that something awful had happened.

"It's here," she cried, "it's here."

What she was saying didn't register, and I must have looked totally bewildered because she went on, enunciating slowly: "The letter arrived today. I put it on your desk."

"The letter," I gasped. "It's here."

I streaked up the stairs into my room and stopped cold in front of my desk. There it was, a delicate pink envelope, addressed to me in lovely handwriting. I dumped my book bag and parka on the floor, and, trying to catch my breath, picked up the letter. The return address was printed in a deep purple, simply Walnut Farms, Scotch Plains, New Jersey. I thought it was the most beautiful envelope I'd ever seen. I slid it open without ripping the flap and withdrew the heavy parchment folded note paper, which was embossed on the front with an elegantly designed initial, *D*. My hands were shaking so hard that I had to rest the note on my desk in order to steady it. There was no date, no greeting. It just began:

Sally—What an incredible surprise to have heard from you! Of course I want to meet you. I've thought about you too, and often wondered how you turned out. It will be wonderful for us to get together. Since you must be going to school, I suppose it'd be best if we met on a Saturday. I have to be in New York on March 8 anyway; Ham is entertaining some South American bankers that evening. Why not meet me at the Empire Club, 10 ½ East 65th Street. It's stuffy, but relatively private. I'll book a table for one o'clock. See you then, darling.

Dee

I read it again, and again, and again, trying to absorb what she'd written. The second line—"Of course I want to meet you"—outweighed everything else. That's all that mattered.

I heard Lucy climbing the stairs and then she was in my room. "Good news, I gather. I can tell by your face."

"She wants to see me!" I exclaimed.

"I'm glad for you, Sally. When are you meeting?"

"On a Saturday."

"Which one?"

It sounds ridiculous, but I had to scan the letter again to find the date.

"March eighth," I answered, and then I gasped, suddenly aware that March 8 was the following day.

"That's tomorrow," Lucy said.

"I just realized that. But that's fine. I mean, I was going to meet Chris and Nina at the record store to pick out Bambi's birthday present, but they can do that without me. Anyhow, I have to meet Delores at one o'clock at the Empire Club."

"Where's that?" Lucy inquired.

"Here, read," I said, and handed her the note.

I watched as she puzzled over the letter. She was frowning slightly as she placed it back on the desk.

"What's wrong?" I asked.

"Nothing, really. It's just that she hasn't given you much time."

"So what?" I couldn't help sounding impatient. "The important thing is she wants to meet me, and as far as I'm concerned, the sooner the better."

"Of course, dear," Lucy said, but her clouded look belied her words.

However, I was much too excited to concern myself with Lucy's reaction. I had other things to think about— like what should I wear to the Empire Club.

Chapter 15.

Fortunately, I was busy every minute for the next eighteen hours. Eric honked the horn announcing his arrival at seven on Friday night. On my way out, I saw George reading the newspaper in the living room, and I told him as calmly as possible that I was meeting Delores for lunch the next day.

"Good luck," he said evenly, and went back to his paper.

I told the news to Eric as soon as I climbed into the car, and the only time I shut up about it was during the concert and afterwards when we stopped with some kids for a pizza. The minute we were alone, I speculated about what Delores would be like, enthused about how anxious she was to meet me, described her perfect handwriting, and on and on. Eric never interrupted, but I finally realized I was overdoing it.

"I'm really a bore," I apologized as he drove up to my house.

"You could never bore me," he assured me. He turned off the motor and pulled me toward him. This was always the most precious part of the evening, just the two of us alone, holding each other and kissing. But I was too hyped up about the next day to fully enjoy being in Eric's arms, and he kidded me about it.

"Think we'll continue this after your rendezvous tomorrow. I like your undivided attention, you know." He was grinning at me, and we both laughed.

"I don't know what I'd do without you, Eric," I said. I gave him a final good-night kiss, and whispered, "I love you."

After I left Eric, I got ready for bed and popped off to sleep amazingly quickly, probably from nervous exhaustion. I didn't awaken until after nine, which gave me three hours to get ready for my appointment. Ordinarily that would be an excessive amount of time, but I barely made it. After I drank some coffee and forced myself to eat a slice of toast, I called Chris and Bambi and Nina. I wanted them to know the details of Delores's letter, and also to discuss in depth what I should wear. The general concensus was that I should wear a skirt rather than pants, and a raincoat rather than a parka.

After trying on several combinations, I finally settled on a dark blue and red plaid skirt, and a navy blue turtleneck. Then I carefully applied blush-on and lip gloss, brushed my hair, and, with the few minutes left before it was time for me to catch the bus, buffed my nails. I was as concerned about how I looked as if I were going to the Junior Prom!

I didn't sit still until I was on the express bus from Riverdale, which would drop me two blocks from my destination. The bus was on schedule and half empty, and I took a window seat in the back. There I could be a people-watcher or take in the scenery. Anything to keep me from going bananas during the forty-minute ride. However, the scenery wasn't particularly spellbinding, and as luck would have it, a young mother with a baby sat opposite me. The baby was a pretty blue-eyed girl with a shock of red hair and a smiley face. The mother had medium brown hair and eyes, and a somber expression. They didn't look at all alike, and I wondered if the baby was adopted. If so, would she one day want to search for her birth mother? Would her adoptive parents help her? This line of thought didn't help my state of nerves, and I closed my eyes so that I would stop staring at them. But no matter how hard I tried, I couldn't turn off my mind.

My head buzzed with questions. Would Delores like me? Would she be disappointed? What if she didn't want her husband to know about me? Would she decide it was best not to see me again? I tormented myself with these questions the entire ride, but finally we arrived at my stop, two blocks from Sixty-fifth Street. It was a crisp sunny day—a good omen, if you believe in weather signs—and I walked briskly to number 10 ½.

The entrance to the Empire Club was so unobtrusive that I almost passed it by. It looked like every other stately brownstone on the block, distinguished only by a small brass plaque on the door with the initials *E. C.* The door was magically opened by a uniformed doorman, who bowed slightly. "Good afternoon, Miss," he greeted me.

"Good afternoon," I said, trying to adjust my eyes to the dark interior.

"Cloakroom's over there. You can check your coat." He tilted his head toward the left.

I thanked him and headed in the direction he'd indicated.

The large foyer was furnished with heavy mahogany Victorian pieces and dimly lit by a crystal chandelier. There were several people waiting around, most of them standing, but some sitting on straight-backed chairs. Without appearing too obvious, I anxiously looked them over. There was no one under the age of fifty, and they all seemed dressed alike, the women in conservative dark suits with frilly blouses, and the men in pinstripes, their wing-tipped shoes shined to a brilliant gloss. They looked like a special species of penguin.

I checked my coat and then ducked into a door that was marked DAMES. I washed my hands, combed my hair, and, taking one final look in the mirror over the sink, said to myself, "Here goes."

The grandfather clock in the foyer chimed one o'clock. There was still no sign of Delores, so I walked toward the dining room. The maitre d' had just returned to his post at the entrance after seating a group of people.

"Are you meeting someone?" he asked.

"Yes," I murmured. "Mrs. Brant."

"Let's see," he said, poring over an oversized appointment book that listed all the reservations.

It seemed to take him an agonizingly long time, and I finally asked, "Is she here?"

"Hmmm. Yes, yes." Another interminable pause, then, "Right over there in the corner."

I knew the proper thing was for him to lead the way, but I couldn't wait. I dashed over to Delores's table. She didn't see me right away, which gave me a chance to look at her unobserved. My first thought was that she was beautiful. Her straight auburn hair was incredibly silky, her sand-colored skin was flawless, and her brown eyes had thick long lashes. I was practically standing on top of her, but she was too absorbed in her own thoughts to

122

notice me. I didn't know what to say, so in order to get her attention, I cleared my throat. That did the trick!

"Sally," she shrieked. She leapt up and threw her arms around me, not the least bit concerned that our scene might shake up the penguins, who must have thought we'd flipped out.

I hugged her back, and muttered her name, "Delores." I felt awkward and self-conscious, but Delores behaved as though a reunion with a fifteen-year-old daughter whom she hadn't seen since she was two days old was an every-day occurrence.

"You're so pretty!" she exclaimed, holding me away from her so that she could appraise me.

"You think so?" I replied, too shy to tell her how beautiful I thought she was.

"But why wouldn't you be," she laughed, "since you are my daughter."

I was delighted to think that we looked alike—same size and coloring, if nothing else.

"We have a lot of catching up to do," she said as we sat down.

"I know."

The waiter arrived and handed us some menus.

"We'd better order, darling. I have a fitting at two, which I simply couldn't change. What would you like?"

"Don't know." I was slightly stunned that we'd only have an hour together, and couldn't think about food.

"The chicken salad here is divine. How about it?"

"Fine."

"And coffee."

"Yes, Delores." I was so overwhelmed by her that if she had suggested Janitor-in-a-Drum I would have ordered that as well.

When the waiter disappeared, she leaned toward me and said, "You must call me Dee. All my friends do."

"Okay, Dee," I agreed.

"I can't tell you, Sally, how relieved I am to see what a lovely girl you are. The people who raised you must be very nice."

"They are. Lucy and George are wonderful."

For the next thirty minutes, she quizzed me about my school, my girlfriends, Eric, what Lucy and George did, where I lived. I can't say I was ever completely at ease, but I answered her questions. Meanwhile I tried to memorize every detail about how she looked. She was wearing a soft brown suit and a beige jewel-necked silk blouse. A wafer-thin gold watch hung from an exquisite tiny-link chain around her neck. I thought she was perfectly dressed, and I wondered if taste was inherited. I hoped so.

I was dying to hear about Dee's life, and I tried desperately to think up a way to approach the subject without sounding fresh, when she unexpectedly said, "You haven't asked me a thing about myself. Aren't you interested?"

"I can't wait to hear about you," I exclaimed, wondering if she was clairvoyant.

"Well," she began, glancing at her watch pendant, "I have time to tell you the highlights. I suppose you'd like to hear about your father."

"Yes, tell me everything." I wasn't sure until that moment that she would ever tell me about him, but Dee was perfectly willing to talk about her past, almost as though she were describing someone else.

"Let me assure you, Sally, he was an okay guy—good-looking, intelligent, but just too young to cope with being a father."

"Where did you meet him?"

"We went to the same high school, but he was two

years ahead of me and we didn't start going out until he was in his first year of college. Before that, he never looked at me. But then one summer vacation—the end of my junior year—someone fixed us up and we started going out. I was so flattered by his attention that I would have done anything to keep him interested. However, when he found out I was pregnant, and I insisted on having the baby, he told me he never wanted to see me again. My family barely tolerated me after that, and only my sister stood by me.''

''Could you finish school?''

''I had to quit in the middle of the year, but after you were born, I managed to get my degree by taking a few credits at night. I still lived with my family, because I had no choice, but as soon as I got my diploma and taught myself typing and steno, I found a job and moved in with three girls who were living in Greenwich Village.''

''That must have been rough.''

''It wasn't easy, but I'm a survivor. And I was assured that you were being adopted by a couple who were desperate to have children. The only other thing I knew about them was that your adoptive father was a schoolteacher, and that meant he must like kids.''

''When did you meet your husband?''

''I had several jobs, but my last one was in a Wall Street investment firm, where I was an executive secretary. Ham was a client, and he had a lot of dealings with my boss, Mr. Hess. One night they kept me working until after seven o'clock, and Ham was so apologetic that he offered to take me and Mr. Hess out to dinner. My boss had to get home, but Ham insisted that I join him. Ham is much older than I am—he's almost fifty—and I didn't think of him at all romantically. But he was very charming, very rich, recently divorced, and lonely.''

"You liked him, didn't you?" I had idealized Dee, and I didn't want to think of her as marrying just for money.

"Of course I liked him. He's a sweetie."

"Does he know about me?"

"He knows my entire history. I couldn't marry someone and not tell him about my past."

I was so riveted by Dee's story that I didn't notice the waiter had cleared away our plates and was hovering over us until he spoke.

"What would you like for dessert, Mademoiselles?"

"The crepes suzettes are heaven, Sally. Would you like them?"

"Love them," I answered, wanting the waiter to go away so Dee would continue.

"We were married three years ago and live in Scotch Plains, as you know. We have two children."

"Two children!" That was a shocker.

"Ham, Jr., is two, and the baby Abigail is nine months."

"I have a half-sister and -brother," I mused.

"They're adorable," Dee bragged unabashedly.

"I'm sure," I said, feeling a ridiculous pang of jealousy.

"You'll have to come visit us." She was so offhand, I wasn't sure if she meant it.

"Would your husband approve?"

"Of course he'd approve. He lets me do anything I want—even bring stray dogs to the house."

I tried to overlook the comparison, and remarked as matter-of-factly as possible, "I'd love to visit you."

"When does your spring vacation begin?"

"March twenty-third."

"That's perfect. You could come for ten days, because April second we're going to Europe."

"You really want me to come?"

"I wouldn't ask you if I didn't mean it. It's a little early for swimming—we don't fill the pool until the end of May—but there's tennis if you want to play, and you can have one of the ponies to ride while you're staying with us.''

''Sounds terrific!''

''The children won't get in your way because Nanny takes complete care of them.''

''I wouldn't mind if they did. I love kids.''

''You'll have to check it out with Lucy and George, but I can't see why they'd disapprove. I'm not about to kidnap you.'' She laughed and waved the waiter over for the bill.

''I'm sure they'll approve.'' I knew Lucy would, anyway, and I didn't want to jinx anything by being hesitant.

''Well then, unless I hear from you to the contrary, I'll expect you March twenty-third. There's a bus that leaves from the Port Authority building at nine-thirty every day. I'll meet you at the Scotch Plains depot.''

''What'll I bring to wear?'' This was probably the most important visit of my life, and I felt stupid worrying about clothes.

''Don't worry about that. You and I are the same size, and I can always fill in your wardrobe.''

She signed the bill that the waiter had brought, and pushed back her chair. ''I have to run off,'' she apologized. ''My dressmaker goes berserk when I'm late.''

I followed her out of the dining room and then told her I had to get my coat. ''It was wonderful meeting you,'' I said.

''Wonderful meeting you too, darling. And do try and make it for the twenty-third.''

''I'll try as hard as I can.''

She gave me a fast hug and then rushed out of the door, which the doorman held open for her. I stood there mesmerized, watching her leave, and it wasn't until a rather portly man on his way out accidentally crashed into me that I knew for sure the whole reunion hadn't been a dream.

"So sorry, young lady," the man apologized. "I almost knocked you over."

"That's all right," I assured him. "Everything is perfectly all right."

Chapter 16.

As I predicted, Lucy was agreeable about me visiting Dee. If she had any misgivings, she didn't let on. George, true to form, didn't give me an argument, but I could tell he wasn't pleased. However, I was too excited to let anything cloud my joyful expectations. My friends—this time I was leaving them instead of the other way around—were all unqualifiedly happy for me. Eric even offered to drive me to the Port Authority building the morning of the twenty-third.

He picked me up at eight-thirty and came into the house to help me with my suitcase. His being there made my saying good-bye to Lucy and George a lot easier. I would be gone less than two weeks, and less than a hundred miles away, but there was a bittersweet quality to my leaving. No one actually came out and said it, but the unspoken truth was that emotionally we might be saying good-bye for much longer than ten days—perhaps forever.

When we arrived at the bus depot, Eric helped me lug my suitcase out of the trunk of the car. Then, in spite of horns honking, and a traffic cop yelling at us that the No Standing sign meant what it said, Eric folded me in his arms and gave me a long good-bye kiss.

"Good luck," he breathed in my ear. "Don't forget I love you."

"Me you," I whispered back.

"Move it, buddy," the policeman shouted. "Your love-making is causing a traffic jam."

"Sorry, officer," Eric said, and flashed that smile that could melt even a traffic cop's heart.

I smiled all the way to the ticket window, thinking how lucky I was at how things had turned out. In fact, I found myself smiling all the way to Scotch Plains. The bus ride was thoroughly enjoyable, even though the scenery was flat and uninteresting most of the trip. It held a special charm for me, because it meant I was getting closer to my destination. Time passed very quickly while I daydreamed about what it would be like to live on an estate for ten days. Then I fantasized about who Dee would bring with her to meet me at the bus depot. Perhaps Ham, Jr., and Abigail, with their Nanny. Or maybe she'd prefer to come alone, so that we'd have a little time by ourselves.

Several people got off at my stop, and while the driver opened the baggage space, I looked around for Dee. There was no sign of her anywhere, and I had a moment of panic that perhaps she'd forgotten her invitation, or maybe she'd forgotten me altogether.

"Which is yours, young lady?" the driver asked.

I pointed out my light blue case and he handed it to me.

"Thank you," I mumbled distractedly.

The people around me drifted off, and the bus driver climbed back into the bus and drove away. I thought I'd look for a phone and try calling the Brant residence, when a jolly-looking Irishman pulled up to the curb in a chocolate-brown four-door Mercedes and beeped the horn in order to get my attention. Then he jumped out and I saw he was wearing a chauffeur's uniform.

"You looking for Mrs. Brant?" he asked.

I was the only one around, so I knew he was addressing me.

"Yes," I answered. "Where is she?"

"She couldn't get out of her golf game this morning; it's the opening of Ladies Day at the country club. I'm Mike, her driver, and I've come to collect you."

I couldn't hide my disappointment and choked up. Mike couldn't help noticing.

"She'll be back for lunch, I'm sure," he consoled me. "Meanwhile, you can get settled."

"Sure," I said, as he took my suitcase from me and tossed it on the front seat of the car. Then he held the back door open for me, and I climbed in, pretending I was used to chauffeur-driven cars.

"How far are we from Walnut Farms?" I inquired.

"About twenty minutes. Just sit back and relax."

I tried to do just that, and not worry about hurt feelings as we sped along a main road. Mike chatted nonstop, and when we turned off the highway, I had learned that he and his wife, Mary, had worked for the Brants for three years. Mary was the cook. They were a wonderful family, except they entertained a little too often; however, they compensated for that by going out a lot, and taking at least three or four trips a year. "If it weren't for Nanny, who thinks she owns those children, the job would be ideal."

We had been driving along a side road where the acreage became more cultivated and the houses more stately with each succeeding mile. "Another few minutes," Mike interrupted himself in the middle of telling me about Bonnie, the upstairs maid, whom he described as something out of an English novel.

We'd come to a private wooded roadway, and Mike made a sharp turn. "This is where their property begins."

"All this?" I was thunderstruck at the amount of land.

"Guarantees privacy." Mike knew I was impressed.

"Who'll the kids play with?"

"Have to be imported, I guess."

We followed the winding gravel road for at least a mile, and the trees became less dense so that I could see a tennis court on one side, and a stable on the other. I didn't want to appear like a bumpkin, but when the house first came into view all I could say was "Wow!" It was a humungus contemporary structure, a combination of fieldstone and glass, in a magnificent rustic setting.

"Like it?" Mike had driven around the circular driveway to the entrance.

"Wow," I repeated.

He beeped the horn and a round, pink-cheeked woman, middle-aged like Mike, with unruly brown curly hair and wearing a full-length apron, came out of the house.

"This is my wife, Mary," Mike told me.

"We've been waiting for you, Miss Sally," she said with the trace of an Irish brogue. She shook my hand warmly and made me feel welcome, although being called "Miss Sally" made me very uncomfortable.

Minutes later, Bonnie appeared. I knew it was Bonnie from Mike's description. It was hard to tell her age, but she was probably younger than she looked. She was dressed in a spotless pink uniform, her straight brown hair held back with a single barette.

We exchanged hellos when Mike introduced us, and then she said, picking up my bag, "I'll show you to your room, Miss Sally."

I cringed at her calling me "Miss" too, but thought it might be rude to ask everyone to just call me Sally. Mary took my coat, which I'd slipped off, and hung it in a closet while I looked around.

The spacious entry hall was decorated with a ficus tree and baskets of fresh flowers and three modern paintings—a Picasso, a Milton Avery, and a swim scene by David Hockney. I was sure they were originals. I wanted to look at them carefully, but Bonnie was already leading the way to the stairs. We had to pass by the living room, and after one glance, I had to stop. "Wait," I called to her, and peered around. I've never been all that interested in decorating, but this was awesome. Everything, the over-stuffed couch and sofa, even the thick piled rug, was white. There were touches of red—a profusion of pillows and a couple of pull-up chairs were covered in lipstick red—which made the white effect even more spectacular. A large stone fireplace surrounded by ceiling-high book shelves covered one entire wall.

"Wow!" I murmured for the third time in less than thirty minutes.

"Like it?" Bonnie asked. She had one foot on the stairs.

"Looks like something out of a magazine. It's perfect."

"Should be. Mrs. Brant has it redone every year. I just about get used to it, and zap! it's all changed."

"Really?" The whole idea of changing one bit of the decor was mind-boggling. "What color scheme was here before?"

"Last year, which was when I came, the walls were deep brown, and everything else was cinnamon, with yellow accessories. When she redid, the old still looked brand-new.''

I had trouble tearing myself away, but Bonnie had started climbing the stairs and I caught up with her.

"You'll be staying in the blue and white room. It's the guest room reserved for one visitor; it only has one bed."

She turned left at the top of the stairs, and I followed her into a corner room that was flooded with sunlight. And there was no question that this was the blue and white room, down to the pale blue phone that graced the night table next to the canopied bed. The draperies, the bedspread and canopy, the flounce on the dressing table were made of the same blue and white pattern. There was a light blue deep-piled rug on the floor that looked like it had never been stepped on. The dresser, mirror, rocking chair, and desk were all white wicker and so flawless that they must have been newly purchased or freshly painted. The walls were covered with photographs, beautiful close-ups of flowers and horses.

"Did Mrs. Brant do these?" I asked.

"It's her hobby. When she's not playing golf or cards, she takes pictures."

"Amazing," I said, wondering if there was such a thing as a photography gene.

Bonnie had rested my suitcase on a luggage rack in the corner, and started to take out my things. "I'll hang these up for you," she offered. "Might need some pressing."

"I can do it," I said, embarrassed by being waited on.

"Then I'll help," she insisted, and went into the closet and brought out a bunch of velvet-covered hangers.

"I don't have that much," I laughed. I held up two skirts and two blouses. "Just these and some jeans and some sweaters."

"That's something, anyhow." She took them from me and carefully placed them on the hangers.

"Now, I suppose you want to meet your brother and sister."

I was astounded that she referred to Ham, Jr., and Abigail that way. I hadn't quite prepared myself for how Dee would describe me to her staff and her friends, and it came as a surprise—and also a relief—that she hadn't hedged.

"Yes, I'd love to meet them."

"I suppose you want to wash up first."

I wasn't sure if that was a hint or a warning, but I took her advice and washed up and combed my hair in the bathroom that had a double sink, enclosed shower, and a dropped tub. I wasn't a bit surprised to see that the color motif was carried out, including the pale blue bar of soap and the blue lucite box of tissues.

When I came out of the bathroom, Bonnie was putting the rest of my things in the dresser. "That's better," she said, glancing sideways at me. Did she mean me or the fact that she'd finished unpacking? It didn't really matter, but I was beginning to see that Bonnie was a master of double meanings.

"Follow me," she instructed. "We have to catch them before their lunch and naps."

"I gather Nanny is very strict." I was inviting her opinion.

"She's something else," she answered noncommittally, as we walked down the long hallway. "The children's suite is at the end."

We'd come to the end of the hall, and Bonnie rapped on one of three doors. "Come in, come in," Nanny instructed. We entered and I saw Nanny, plain, pinched, and as

135

starched as her immaculate white uniform, sitting in a straight-backed chair, surveying her charges.

This was obviously Ham, Jr.'s room, equipped like a nursery school with every conceivable toy, including a built-in swing, a portable slide, and even an elaborate set of electric trains that he was much too young to enjoy.

Ham, a sturdy little dark-haired fellow with a turned-up nose, was in the corner, constructing something out of giant-sized blocks. He looked at me indifferently for a brief moment and then turned back to his job. Abigail, a round little bundle with fair skin and practically no hair, was lying on her back in a playpen, idly flicking a mobile of silver shapes that was fastened to the edge of the pen.

I stood just inside the door, trying to adjust to the idea that these were my blood relatives—my brother and sister. The whole scene was unreal, and I would have stayed glued to the spot if Bonnie hadn't tapped me gently on the shoulder and said, "They don't bite."

"You must be Sally," Nanny surmised. "We heard you were coming. Hamilton, come over here and say hello."

"Oh, don't bother him," I protested.

"If he doesn't learn manners now, he never will," Nanny snapped, and again called him over.

Ham reluctantly tore himself away from his construction, and extended his hand.

"Hello," he mumbled, without looking at me, and then scooted off.

"It's a start," Nanny remarked. "You can go look at the baby now, Sally, but she's been fussing all morning so I'd rather you didn't pick her up."

I walked quietly to the playpen, leaned over, and smiled at Abigail, who gave me back a big smile. It was hard to believe that such a sweet-looking baby would give anyone any trouble, and I did have to fight my impulse to touch her.

"They're darling, both of them," I said as I backed away.

Nanny didn't bother to answer, except by suggesting we leave so that she could get them ready for lunch.

I was so intimidated by Nanny that I didn't dare ask if I could come back later to see them. But after we'd left the room, Bonnie volunteered the information that "visiting hours" were between three and four, if nothing else was scheduled.

"She's very rigid," I observed. "But what about their mother?"

"Mrs. Brant is allowed to break the rules, of course, but she's awfully busy."

"Busy? She doesn't work or anything." I couldn't help comparing her with Lucy who, except for an occasional babysitter, had taken complete care of me.

"She has a lot of social obligations," Bonnie explained.

"I see," I said, although I questioned Dee's priorities. Were golf and cards more important than her children?

We'd come to the top of the stairs, and Bonnie said it was time for her to help in the kitchen. "Mrs. Brant should be here shortly, and she wants lunch on the patio. Meanwhile, why don't you just wander around."

"I'll do that," I said, and thanked her for all her help.

Once I was on my own, I ambled around the beautifully landscaped gardens in the back of the house, and then made my way to the stables. I introduced myself as "Sally" to the raw-boned young man who looked like a transplanted Western cowboy, and told him I was a house guest. He told me to call him Jake, and then showed me the three riding horses and two ponies, which were in his charge. He was shocked to learn that I'd never been on a horse.

"It's easy. I'll teach you how to ride in a couple of hours. Main thing is to not be afraid."

"Maybe tomorrow?"

"Sure thing. We have a ring over there where I'm already walking Ham, Jr., around on his pony. If he can do it, so can you."

"Thanks for the compliment," I laughed.

We seemed to have exhausted any further conversation, and I watched in silence while Jake currycombed a glistening chestnut. After a few minutes, I heard a car swish by on the road, and I told Jake I had to leave and would see him tomorrow.

I ran back to the house, where I saw Dee getting out of a dark red Porsche.

"Dee," I yelled just as she was about to disappear into the house.

"Sally, darling, you made it. I'm so glad." She threw her arms around me with genuine enthusiasm, and told me to come upstairs while she showered and changed.

"Your house is so beautiful."

"I hope you enjoy it. Did Bonnie get you settled?"

"Yes, and I got to meet Ham, Jr., and Abigail."

"Your timing must have been right," she quipped, "otherwise Nanny would never have given you an audience."

I could see that Dee, if no one else, had a sense of humor about Nanny.

"I'll only be a minute," Dee said, going into the bathroom. "You can relax on the chaise lounge and read a magazine."

I sat gingerly on the edge of the puffed-up chaise, too fascinated by the decor to think of looking at a magazine.

The master bedroom was huge, one wall consisting of a floor-to-ceiling window that commanded a view of the pool, the tennis court, and the fields and forests beyond. This room was done in a delicate floral quilted chintz, and, except for a book that was left open on the night table that separated the twin beds, didn't look lived in.

After a few minutes, Dee came out of the shower wrapped in a luxurious bath sheet, opened a walk-in closet, and pulled out a dark red wool shift. I could see that the clothes in the closet were precisely arranged according to style and color, skirts, blouses, and jackets on one side, and dresses and gowns on the other.

She dressed quickly, talking all the time. She apologized for not being able to meet me, but added, "Actually, there was a luncheon, but I didn't stay for that. I told my friends that I wanted to have lunch with you."

"That was good," I said, trying to overlook how unhappy I was that she hadn't picked me up at the depot.

I followed her downstairs to the patio, which was enclosed with sliding glass doors. It was too cool to dine al fresco, but this was almost the same, because the patio extended beyond the house so that it bordered on the manicured gardens. Bonnie served us crabmeat salad and homemade strawberry tarts and coffee with double-rich whipped cream. The luxury was overwhelming, and surpassed all my expectations.

"I haven't made a lot of plans for you, Sally, but I can tell you're very self-sufficient."

"Think so," I said, and told her I'd already met Jake and he was going to give me a riding lesson the next day.

"That's great, because the private schools don't begin their vacation until next week, so there aren't too many of my friends' kids around now."

"By the way, I'm glad that everyone here knows I'm your daughter. Do your friends know too?"

"Yes. I wouldn't dream of lying about that. When anyone asks questions, I simply tell them you're a part of my former life and circumstances forced me to give you up. That usually shuts them up."

I thought it was wonderful that Dee was so forthright and accepting of me. I probably just didn't understand the importance of the opening of Ladies Day, and after all, we would have ten days together.

I was finally beginning to relax and enjoy myself when Dee spoke to Bonnie, who had just finished pouring us a second cup of coffee.

"Make sure the card table is set up in the den, Bonnie. My friends should be here any minute."

"Yes, ma'am," Bonnie said.

"And please bring down my handbag that I left in my room and tell Mike that Sally will be going to town soon."

"You're playing cards this afternoon?" I tried to keep my voice from trembling.

"Yes, darling. It's my regular bridge game. I was sure you wouldn't mind, and I thought it would give you a good opportunity to go shopping. Mike will drive you, and you can use my charge cards."

"I couldn't do that without you," I protested.

"I insist! There's a marvelous Tops and Bottoms shop where all the kids go. And there's Saks, and Lord and Taylor. Whatever you want."

"But Dee, I'd rather wait for you."

"To tell the truth, Sally, I hate shopping for other people, but you know I want to buy you something. You'd be doing me a favor."

"Okay," I said, feeling totally confused. "If you really want me to."

The doorbell rang then, and I followed Dee into the hall, where she proudly introduced me to her friends. They gushed over me briefly, and then went off to the den. Dee hung behind, took out the charge cards from the bag that Bonnie had brought downstairs, and told me to have fun.

As I settled into the back seat, I wanted to look forward to a shopping expedition where I didn't have to worry about how much money I spent. But no matter how hard I tried, I felt grim. I knew Dee, in her way, was being nice to me, but I had never felt so alienated in my life.

Chapter 17.

My first five days at Walnut Farms I considered an orientation period. Between learning to ride, hitting some tennis balls with the pro at the country club, tagging along with Dee while she played golf, and having lunch with her friends, who mainly gossiped about people I didn't know, I was kept busy. Nanny was so protective of Ham, Jr., and Abigail that I felt I was always interrupting their schedule and therefore never got to know them.

Ham, Sr., was exactly as Dee described him: a sweetie. He was a balding portly man, with a benign manner. Dee told me privately that he was a wonderful husband—which I gathered meant she could do whatever she wanted—but that he was a deadly businessman—which enabled her to do whatever she wanted. During the cocktail hour, before dinner guests arrived or they went out, Ham always asked me if I'd had a nice day. The problem was, no matter how

I tried to respond without being boring, his eyes glazed over. On several occasions he took a pad out from his pocket and scribbled down a note to himself. His mind was always on business.

The first Saturday I was there, Delores arranged for me to be invited to a party given by one of her friends' kids. I was a little nervous about going because I wouldn't know anybody, but Dee told me that "this adorable boy," Carlton Gifford, who was a freshman at Princeton, would pick me up and take me home.

That made me even more apprehensive, because I'd never been out with a college man. Still, it all sounded very glamorous. Dee and Ham had rushed off to a theater party in New York before I got ready, and I wasn't sure what to wear. If only I could have consulted Nina and Bambi and Chris I would have felt a lot more confident. Not only would they have advised me on what to wear, but also on how to talk to a college man. I was really on my own!

I decided on a white angora sweater and a wine-colored skirt that I had bought at Tops and Bottoms. It must have been a good choice, because when Carlton arrived in his blue Maserati and I opened the door for him, the first thing he said to me was, "Smashing!"

Carlton was just about the most preppy-looking guy I'd ever seen, from his light blue button-down collared shirt to his dark brown loafers. He was also very cute—curly blond hair and blue eyes—and I wondered how I'd feel if Eric was fixed up with someone he found attractive.

As soon as we got in the car, Carlton confided that he was pleasantly surprised with his assignment for the evening.

"You mean me?"

"Yeah, you. I was doing my mother a big favor. She's a friend of Dee's, and someone had to take care of you."

"Thanks a lot," I said sarcastically.

"Only kidding, kid. You're really cute. A little on the young side, I'm told, but I'll make allowances."

I wasn't quite sure how to handle this college man, so of course I came up with the wrong answer. "I'll be sixteen in June."

"You would have fooled me," he said, a remark I could have interpreted several different ways. He was grinning, though, and I decided not to take him so seriously.

Actually, he was easy to talk to, mainly because he did all the talking. By the time we reached Alison's house, where the party was given, he'd already told me he was majoring in economics, had made the freshman tennis team, planned to go to law school, and then to work in his father's firm.

"Why struggle if I don't have to? Right, Sal?"

"Why not?" I asked. But we had arrived at Alison's and he wasn't a bit interested in any ideas I might have on the subject. He led the way to her door.

The house was a large split-level with a huge family room where taped music blared out at us as soon as we entered. It reminded me of all the parties I'd been to in Riverdale, the only difference being that I didn't know anyone. Alison, a small, vivacious, short-haired brunette, was the perfect hostess. She introduced me to half the kids—there were at least thirty—and everyone was friendly, although I definitely felt like an outsider. I mean, they had probably all grown up together, had all the same teachers, belonged to the same country club. I wasn't a wallflower for a minute, but I missed Eric more than ever. I didn't see much of Carlton all evening. He seemed to be spreading his charm all over the place, and I was an occasional recipient. Our longest conversation took place when Carlton told me to get ready to leave because he had to get up early to work on his serve.

On the way home, he stopped the car at the edge of the road before we made the turn off for Walnut Farms. He was a reckless driver, and I thought that perhaps he'd lost his bearings.

"What's wrong?" I asked.

"Nothing's wrong." He grabbed me around the waist and pulled me toward him.

"Hey, Carlton, it was really nice of you to pick me up and everything, but this is—"

"This is my reward, you might say."

"That's insulting!" I tried to push him off, but he was too strong for that. But I did succeed in turning my face away when he tried to kiss me, so that his mouth landed on my ear.

"Maybe you *are* too young for me," he barked angrily.

"Has nothing to do with age. We hardly know each other."

"How do you expect us to get friendly if you're going to put on the Girl Scout act?"

"I'm no Girl Scout, and besides, you have to get up early to practice your serve, remember?"

"I just thought I'd give you a break and kiss you good night. You don't know what you're missing." He released me then, revved up the motor, and burned up the road the rest of the way.

His conceit was so overwhelming that I was speechless. We drove in silence, which I didn't break until we came to my door. I let myself out as he remained behind the wheel, and then I said, "Thanks for the lift."

"Don't mention it," he muttered without looking at me. "And when you grow up in six or eight years, call me."

That night, as I got ready for bed, I felt lonelier than

ever. I had no one to talk to. I tried to convince myself that things would be better in the morning when I saw Dee.

Dee always had breakfast in bed, so I didn't see her until about nine-thirty, when she popped her head in the breakfast room where I was having French toast. She was wearing golf clothes, so I knew she was heading for the club.

"Hi, Sal. Want to come with me? I'm in a foursome that starts in fifteen minutes."

"No thanks, Dee. I think I'll go riding."

"Don't blame you. That's more fun than watching me dig up the course." The one thing I had learned for sure about Dee was that she was never insulted if I didn't choose to spend time with her. "By the way, how was the party?" she asked.

"It was fun."

"And wasn't I right about Carlton? All the girls flip over him."

"Well, he is cute looking, but—"

Before I could finish saying "but probably the most conceited boy I'd ever met," she glanced at her wristwatch and shrieked, "I have to run, darling. If we don't tee off on time, especially on Sunday, we can lose our place altogether. I'll see you at dinner tonight."

I called after her, "Have a good game," but she was off so quickly I wasn't sure if she heard me, or if she cared.

There were only a couple of days left of my fairyland vacation, and I wanted to make the most of them. That morning I rode around Walnut Farms by myself. Jake trusted me to go off alone, but cautioned me not to overdo the cantering—a new accomplishment I found exhilirating. He told me I was a very apt pupil and that in another week he would have me jumping. I was surprised how delighted I was to tell him that I wouldn't be there another week.

I trotted off toward the fields beyond the tennis courts, where a bridle path had been carved out of the forest. I slowed my horse to a walk and tried to soak in the brilliantly clear morning and shed my feeling of desolation.

Since I was exactly where I wanted to be, since Dee and Ham had been very nice, and since I'd never been treated so royally in my life, it was hard to understand my discontent. Still, I couldn't wait for the next two days to be over. I'd thought a lot about Eric and Nina, and longed to talk to them, and would have loved to share everything I was doing with them. Also, it suddenly hit me that I desperately missed Lucy and George. They cared about me more than anything in the world, and I cared as much for them, but I had never realized it until this separation.

Dee was my birth mother, but I knew that Lucy was my *real* mother. I could never feel deeply about Dee because, even though she was fun and generous, she was only interested in herself. I had fantasized that there would be a natural bond between us and that we would love each other deeply because by the laws of nature we belonged to one another, but it simply wasn't true.

The morning I was to leave, everyone came outside to see me off. Even Nanny appeared with Ham, Jr., and Abigail, and I was allowed to kiss them good-bye. I shook hands with Mary and Bonnie, and thanked them for taking such good care of me. Nanny patted me on the shoulder, and then whisked the children away. Ham, Sr., embraced me awkwardly, making me feel more than ever that I was like his wife's maiden aunt whom he had been instructed to tolerate.

Dee, gay as always, told me it was fantastic having me

visit. "You can come again whenever you want. We're going to Europe, you know, and after that we'll be doing a lot of weekending. But let's be sure and have lunch in the fall."

"That'll be great," I said, and meant it. I could accept a casual relationship with Dee, and see her in perspective, because now I was going home to the people who meant the most to me: my *real* parents. The Brants' lavish estate, the impeccable staff, the lack of concern about money could never be a substitute for what Lucy and George gave me—their unqualified, unselfish love.

Chapter 18.

Lucy and George knew I would be coming home that Tuesday, but they weren't sure what time. I'd taken a West Side express bus and then walked from my stop in Riverdale to my house. I heard the familiar sound of the electric saw and went around to the back where George was cutting a plank of wood, probably for an outdoor table he'd been threatening to make for the past three summers.

"Hi, Daddy," I called to him—three times before he heard me.

He turned off the saw and stared at me for one full minute as though he couldn't believe his eyes, and then he whispered, "You're back."

"I'm back," I echoed. I dropped my suitcase and ran into his arms.

"Sally, Sally, Sally," he murmured, hugging me to him. "I've missed you more than you'll ever know."

"You mean you're not angry at me anymore?" No matter how hard I tried, I couldn't forget how cool he'd been the weeks before I left.

"I was never really mad at you. I just had to keep some distance between us because I was scared that I might lose you."

"I knew that would never happen."

"Once you'd actually left the house, I saw things more clearly, and I knew too that the love we had between us wouldn't suddenly disappear just because you found Delores. Even if she fulfilled all your dreams, you'd always belong to us."

"You're right, Daddy. I think if I hadn't met her I would have a cloud of doubt about who I was and where I came from all my life. Now I know, for sure, who I am, and that you and Mother are my family. For the first time, I feel like a complete person."

"I promised Lucy we'd call the minute I laid eyes on you. She's taking the rest of the day off as soon as she hears from us."

"Fantastic. I can't wait to see her."

"Why don't you call her, Sal? She'll be so excited." He picked up my suitcase, and I followed him through the back door to the foot of the stairs, where he put down my bag. Peaches was sunning herself on the windowsill in the living room and allowed me to take her in my arms.

Our house had never looked so cozy and warm, and as I went back into the kitchen and picked up the receiver, I thought how delicious to not have to worry about the staff hovering around.

I asked for Lucy's extension and she picked up immediately. "Mother, I'm back."

"Welcome home, Sally," she said, "welcome home."

Sensitive portraits of young adults...

JUNIPER BOOKS

28

FAWCETT
Brings you the
Best of
JUNIPER

28